THE MURDER MIND

SAM RAVEN
BOOK ELEVEN

BRIAN DRAKE

ROUGH
EDGES
PRESS

The Murder Mind
Paperback Edition
Copyright © 2025 Brian Drake

Rough Edges Press
An Imprint of Wolfpack Publishing
1707 E. Diana Street
Tampa, FL 33610

roughedgespress.com

Paperback ISBN 978-1-68549-555-8
Ebook ISBN 978-1-68549-656-2

This one is for my mother. Her investment in me makes this the most expensive book she's ever owned!

THE MURDER MIND

THE BAR SMELLED OF SWEAT, SMOKE, AND DESPERATION.

It wasn't the worst dive Tracy Donahue ever visited, but it was close. She felt reassured having four tough, armed men watching her back. They were scattered throughout, awaiting her signal of all's well or get out. She planned to give the word through a wireless microphone pinned under the left strap of her dark green tank top.

Men filled the bar, though there were enough women hanging around for Tracy not to be out of place. It was hot in Tangier, and clothing was light all around. The ceiling fans fought a losing battle with the stuffy air; everybody had their share of sweaty skin. None of the patrons seemed bothered as long as the bartenders and roving wait staff kept the beer and liquor flowing.

Everyone had hard faces and visible scars; the bar wasn't a tourist tavern. It was in a corner of Tangier visited by the local cops, because of fights, almost as much as the regulars, who started the fights. It was a bar where you were either a soldier-for-hire—a mercenary—between jobs, or you were somebody looking to hire same. Nobody challenged Tracy because they had no idea which side she represented. Some of the glances cast her way were hopeful. Perhaps she had the job they were looking for after a long dry spell. She didn't care about disappointing them. She saw lust in some of their glances. Others promised violence.

Tracy had a hard appearance, too. She'd seen plenty of violence in her career. To her, last-second life-and-death decisions were as natural as a spreadsheet to an accountant. She could have passed for either side, but she wasn't hiring or looking for work. Tracy Donahue was a CIA officer on a mission. She was there to meet an informant to talk about somebody selling nuclear trigger circuits to a ready client. The buyer wanted to build a nuclear bomb. The seller wanted two million US dollars. Unacceptable. Tracy needed to stop them both.

Tracy passed the tables in the front area and wandered to the middle section where three pool tables filled the space. Cigar and cigarette smoke hung in the air and stung her eyes. She ignored the discomfort. Booths lined the back wall beyond the pool tables, and Tracy spotted the man she'd come to see occupying one of them. He sat alone.

Tracy said, "Our man is here, we are go," without turning her head to her left shoulder strap. Nothing gave away a wire faster; she still made mistakes, but not rookie mistakes. She hoped her team received the message over the loud clientele letting off steam. The informant detached enough to watch everything, but not so hidden nobody noticed if they bothered to look. It didn't mean anything more than he wanted solitude, and the patrons obliged. He was none of their business.

Tracy walked a little faster, her boots thumping on the wood floor. She had a well-muscled, thick frame, long dark hair, and big brown eyes. She stood almost six feet with enough curves to catch even the attention of men who

avoided tall women, and a lot of men indeed avoided tall women, as Tracy's hard knocks dating life proved. She'd tied back her hair; it bounced as she walked. Her sharp jaw and prominent cheekbones made her look like she needed to eat. But the flat line of her lips and general air of disquiet suggested she had more on her mind than her next meal. Only her muscles proved she was more than the average chick. Tonight, Tracy was chasing nuclear material. During her downtime, she pursued another mission, a private effort, much closer to her heart, one she was aware she might never complete. But she spent many nights unable to sleep because of it, so she kept trying.

The informant looked up at her as she reached the booth. He was younger than her. His name was Greg Rayel, and he was heavy and dark-skinned with oily black hair. Half a beer sat in front of him; an empty mug, the traces of foam still visible on the inside, sat off to the side.

"Which one was mine?" Tracy said. She slid into the booth opposite Rayel.

"Sorry," he said.

"I'm sure there's more." Tracy gestured at a passing waitress who only called out, "Hang on," before moving farther away.

Tracy faced the dark-haired man. "Let's have it."

"Deal's happening tonight. Maybe two hours from now."

"What's with the last minute bullshit?"

"Look, it wasn't my idea. They moved up the meet, okay? You got people here, right? You can handle it."

"Never mind. Where?"

The waitress returned but Tracy said, "Forget it," while Rayel reached for one of the back pockets of his jeans. The waitress continued on. Tracy didn't need to tell her team to stand by; they were listening to the conversation as it happened. They'd known the deal wasn't far off, but she thought they had more time. Such was life. They'd have to scramble once she saw what Rayel scrawled on the piece of paper. He unfolded the small square, and she grabbed it out of his hand. He blinked in surprise at the speed of her reach.

She examined the page in the low light. A hand-drawn map. Crisscrossing lines and street names. A large "X" marked a spot outside the city in the hills near Merkala Beach.

"It's a house near the—"

"I get it. All right, come on." Tracy refolded the sheet and slipped it beneath her tank top and under the left cup of her bra. "Let's go."

"Go where?"

"You want to get paid? We have to recover the item first."

"That wasn't—"

"You want the money, do what I tell you," she told him. "Take it or leave it, dude." She left the booth, muttering under her breath—or so it seemed to anybody watching. She gave curt instructions for her team to get their backsides in gear. They had to hustle. She didn't have to look behind her to hear the heavy-set dark-haired informant racing to catch up.

Bringing Rayel along was insurance against a set-up. The change in time set off an alarm in the back of Tracy's mind. If the other side had flipped Rayel and forced him to lead her team into an ambush, he'd have continued to argue. Since he was keeping pace beside her, she decided a trap wasn't in the cards. Rayel wanted to collect his money. The CIA promised a generous payout should he deliver; he appeared to be an eager errand boy.

But there was still plenty to go wrong. There were always variables they couldn't predict or control. She needed to counteract any surprises.

"TARGETS LEAVING THE BAR."

Gorm Bjerre tried not to sound nervous, but his heart was pumping. His voice shook a little. There was a lot to do before the sun rose again. Taking care of the CIA team was pulling resources away from the primary goal, but they had no choice. If they didn't deal with the Americans first, it didn't matter if their deal over the trigger circuits went without a hitch. The Americans would try and stop it. They had to prevent the Americans from ever getting *near* the deal.

He let up on the talk button on the handheld radio, hoping he hadn't held it down too long. Then his team leader spoke.

"Which door?"

"Front and side. They're heading for the van parked around the corner."

"Is Rayel with them?"

Rayel. *The traitor.* Bjerre wanted to slit the man's throat, but the boss said otherwise. They wouldn't have known about Rayel had their inside man at the CIA not told them, albeit at the last minute. He hadn't known until then, he claimed. Bjerre had no reason to think their insider lied. But in the underworld, treachery lurked everywhere.

"He's following behind the woman," Bjerre said.

Gorm Bjerre released the talk button again and waited. A moment passed with no reply, but he didn't prompt his commander. Bjerre watched the CIA team pile into the large black van he and his gun crews had been told to look for. The vehicle matched the photos provided by their insider. The brief flash of streetlight on the woman's face revealed another match to a supplied picture. Gorm Bjerre began to apply pressure to the talk button again. Then the voice of Javier Chistau finally came back over the small speaker.

"I want everyone in position. Get ready to block the street. Assault team, don't miss. We don't know what weapons they may have, and a long gun battle doesn't serve our purposes. Everyone acknowledge."

Bjerre listened as the other crew members replied. Chistau's last order was to him, a curt, "Catch up with me around the block."

Bjerre radioed back, "Okay," and started his car. They were making their move at the right time of night. There was very little street traffic, with most establishments already closed. Only those catering to tourists or "other" city residents, such as the mercenary types in the dive bar, remained open.

But Bjerre, parked between two brick buildings, still checked for traffic before pulling out. He drove slowly at first, his pulse rate still high. The trick was learning not to let the rush control his actions. Instead, he needed to master the rush and make it work for him.

Bjerre was a twenty-three-year-old Norwegian, former university student. He'd quit school to join a group of Marxists activists who wanted to overthrow western capitalism. Most of their comrades spoke against violence and advocated for change by publishing and speaking. Not Chistau's unit, and especially Chistau's boss. They wanted a strict military solution, which meant taking the war to the streets of Europe and beyond. The ragtag group was young and eager. But they didn't have a name yet. Their leader felt a name would jeopardize their mission. If they didn't have a name, the authorities couldn't track them. If they couldn't be tracked, there was no way to stop them. It made sense to Bjerre, but he thought a proper name would bring a sense of pride to the effort. It was an argument for another time.

Now, there was a mission to complete.

TRACY PULLED the passenger door shut. She hurried to punch the address on Rayel's map into the dashboard GPS.

"Will the locals get their act together in time?"

The question came from the man in the driver's seat, Max Mason. Rugged and clean-cut, he was an inch shorter than Tracy.

"They better," she said, hitting the last of the street address into the GPS.

A voice from the back said, "Calling our people now." John Rosen held his cell phone in his left hand while inserting a wireless earpiece into his right ear.

Tracy's team—all five of them—weren't the sole assets deployed to stop the sale of the nuclear triggers. CIA personnel at the US Embassy in Rabat, the capital of Morocco, were also assigned to the task. They were standing by for further instructions. Max Mason had the van in gear and moving when Rosen began updating whoever answered the other end of the line.

The remaining two members of the team worked with speed in the rear of the van. Greg Macedo and Mitch Storey, two veteran CIA officers with almost as much service time as Tracy, began unloading a case of rifles and equipment. They passed the automatic rifles and combat gear forward to their teammates.

Tracy took her Galil ACE Gen II from Rosen as he talked on the phone and placed it between her knees with the muzzle on the floor. The chamber wasn't loaded, but it was an old habit, a safety protocol from her days in the US Army and numerous hops into combat zones via helicopter. The idea was a weapon may discharge during a bumpy flight, go through the roof, and damage the rotors should the rifle be held with the muzzle pointed up. It made more sense to send the errant bullet through the floor of the chopper. She never had the guts to ask if the chopper was any better off with holes in the floor, damage being damage and all that. Deferring to those who outranked her was the better option at the time. But sometimes, she wondered if her superiors would have had the answer. The irony of now overseeing her own crew, and how often she *didn't* know the answers, and needed experience and help from her team, was never far from her thoughts.

Holding the rifle between her knees, and while Max Mason drove, she strapped on a web belt of spare magazines for the ACE.

Rosen ended his call and announced, "No backup."

Tracy snapped around in her seat. "What?"

"The Moroccans found out. They told the embassy to stand down and said this is their problem to deal with. We're to stand down too."

"No!" Tracy said. "We'd have—hang on, I'm calling Graham." Her local handler, Evan Graham, not at the embassy in Radat but at a hotel in Tangier waiting for news, would know the real score.

She reached for her phone while taking a quick scan out

the window. Not a lot of traffic, Max was driving at a good clip. Darkened storefronts and apartment buildings lined either side of the road. They passed through one intersection on a green light, and the next one ahead was green too. She hoped it would stay green. The fewer delays, the better.

She was about to press the button for Evan Graham's number when another car caught her attention. It was crossing parallel to them through the intersection ahead despite the green light. The car screeched to a stop, blocking them. Max Mason let out a curse and slowed; then his foot slammed on the gas pedal, and he yelled for everyone to hold on. He spun the wheel in a hard left turn. Four men emerged from the stopped car—four men with submachine guns—who opened fire.

———

THE FOUR GUNMEN paid no attention to the handful of motorists honking for them to get out of the way. When they started shooting, the honking stopped.

The men weren't Moroccan; they were a mix of white European and Corsican. Young men in their twenties. The oldest was twenty-eight. They aimed at the windshield, but as the van's driver made a sharp left turn, their fusillade smacked into the side. One of the back tires popped as the van completed its turn, and then the shooters had to reload. They smiled because the Americans thought they had a way out. They didn't yet see the second carload of shooters blocking the opposite end of the street.

———

TRACY HATED BEING TALL.

But she *was* glad she hadn't used a seat belt.

She turned her body to drop lower in the footwell but barely cleared the passenger window. Covering the back of her neck with one hand while trying to move her rifle out of the way with the other, she kept her face close to the seat cushion. And she did what any commanding officer does during an attack. She yelled for her crew to get down. The gunfire popped and smacked into the van. The passenger window glass took several hits, spiderwebbing under the impacts, finally breaking. Sharp bits rained on her back and slipped down her tank top. Max Mason screamed, and the van dipped in back as a tire popped, and the van stopped with a sudden jolt and crunch of metal. More rounds hit the body of the vehicle, but few penetrated the steel. It was one saving grace. The shooters weren't using ammunition powerful enough to turn the van into a block of Swiss cheese. But the van wasn't moving. Max wasn't moving. They were stuck. If they didn't find a way to solve their problem, the protection of the van wouldn't stop the enemy for long.

Tracy looked at Max. His right arm was bloody from the hole in his shoulder and the color had already drained from his skin. The bullet had continued into his chest cavity. The van was jammed against the front of another car in the roadway, the occupants of which were running and screaming to the doorway of a closed shop. They huddled low with the man shielding the woman and covering both her body and eyes.

More tires screeched. Tracy saw a second car stopping at the other end of the street. Four more gunmen leaped out.

"Incoming!" she shouted. This time, she grabbed her Galil ACE 5.56mm and smashed out enough of the windshield to take aim. She fired through the hole. The four shooters spread out, returning fire. In the back of the van, Macedo and Story announced the first crew were running toward them.

"Max is hit!" she yelled. "Everybody out!"

She shoved her door open, wincing as incoming fire smacked at the windshield glass and the doorframe. Using the door for cover, she tucked the rifle tight to her shoulder and scanned for a target. The second gun crew remained concealed. She pivoted to engage the first group coming from behind.

Rosen was already out, firing, covering Macedo and Storey as they jumped out the back. Macedo stopped a slug as his feet hit the pavement and he dropped. Storey returned fire as he made his way around the driver's side to Max Mason's door. Tracy fired a burst, swung around to the front again, and fired another salvo. This time, her rounds scored. One of the second group of gunmen rose from behind a car to take the slugs in the chest and neck. He pitched backward with his weapon skidding across the blacktop.

Storey opened the driver's door and dragged Max Mason out. More gunfire crackled as Tracy aimed her rifle at Greg Rayel, the informant, still inside the van and crouched on the floor. His face was twisted in fear, coated with sweat.

"You sold us out!"

"No!" he shouted.

Tracy shot him in the head. Before his body stopped twitching, she was gone, racing around the back of the van, passing Macedo's fallen corpse. Rosen shouted behind her, but gunfire cut off his words. The enemy fire ripped into him. Tracy hit the pavement and rolled for the sidewalk. Storey had Mason lying near the edge of the curb, concealed by a parked car. The gunfire stopped for a moment, but the shooters were yelling to each other, advancing to finish the job.

Tracy braced at the rear of the parked car. Storey directed

his attention to the front; Mason's body lay between them. She could not tell if Mason was alive or not, but the stillness of his body didn't give her any confidence. She reloaded her rifle. A grim determination consumed her as she racked the action. If she wasn't going to make it out of Tangier alive, she'd take as many of the enemy with her as her trigger finger allowed.

3

STOREY TRIED TO SHIELD MASON'S BODY WITH HIS OWN, AND when he tried to protect Tracy at the same time, it cost him his life.

The gunners Storey faced came toward the front of the car, using the sidewalk and street. They coordinated their fire—one let off a burst, then the other, hosing the car. Glass broke. Bullets punched through metal. Storey kept his head down but the longer he did, the closer the enemy came. He shifted his body to block Mason and Tracy while aiming at the gunner on the sidewalk. His weapon chugged a burst and the gunner dropped. But then the gunner's partner seized the moment and shot Storey in the head.

Tracy heard the bullet impact and felt the projectile pass by as bits of Storey struck her. She heard the thump of his body landing on Mason and then rolling onto the sidewalk. Pivoting, she fired a burst at the gunner coming at her from Storey's side. The ones approaching the rear remained under cover. They were letting their teammates make the first approach. There was nothing she could do for her team, but she needed to get away fast. She knew exposing her backside was dangerous, but didn't see any other way. Staying low, she bolted from the car, out of the spotlight of a streetlamp. Gunfire chased her, whining off the building wall to her right. She hurried from the light to the darkness of an alley. At the same time, the second set of gunners opened fire. Their shots chewed up the alley entrance as Tracy merged into the shadows within.

Her left foot slipped.

On a wet puddle, wet garbage, whatever; it didn't matter. All Tracy felt was the sensation of losing traction and falling onto hard concrete. Her breath rushed out of her as she landed, pain flaring through her body. The Galil ACE flew from her grasp and skidded across the ground. More yelling behind her—the gunners coordinating yet again. She crawled using her knees and elbows, ignoring the hurt and trying to get her breath back. The light from the street didn't extend far into the alley, and there were no lights on either alley wall. She felt ahead for her weapon, but the gun wasn't within reach. Panic. Pulse racing. She moved faster. Her left hand bumped the sharp bottom edge of a dumpster. She stifled a cry as the edge ripped at her skin. There was enough of a gap between the concrete and the floor of the dumpster for her weapon to have slid beneath. Footsteps behind her. The enemy was at the alley entrance. She ran her hand beneath the dumpster, found her weapon, and hauled it out. Clutching it close, she rolled onto her back to fire two single shots at the outlines on the sidewalk. The figures ducked back once again.

Still hurt and trying to suck in enough air to not pass out, Tracy began jogging toward the other end of the alley. She stayed close to one of the walls, but not so close to disturb the piles of trash stacked on both sides. The wooden pallets. Broken bits of miscellany. Junk serving no purpose.

A cramp hit her in the belly; Tracy slowed, stopped. She

stretched out behind a pile of trash to watch the entrance of the alley. She gasped hard, sweat dripping into her eyes. The darkness played tricks on her mind as tunnel vision also interfered. She sensed threats other than the gunners. Tracy wiped sweat from her face and stole a glance behind her. The opposite end wasn't far away. She saw light. A portion of an empty street. No discernible threats. But what waited on the opposite side of the alley? She had no backup, no contact with her handler, no transportation...

GORM BJERRE SWUNG his car in a sharp left turn, screeching the tires, and slowed. He tried to see into each alley on the left side of the street, but the line of parked cars obscured his view. He stopped. He hated the streetlamps. They'd benefit both him *and* the woman, so he had to gain the upper hand fast. He had to see *her* before she saw *him*.

"Where are you?" said Javier Chistau over the radio.

Bjerre updated the team leader, who said, "I'm coming to you from the other end. She'll come to us eventually."

"Copy." Bjerre reached under his jacket for the pistol he carried in a shoulder harness. He checked the gun by easing back the slide. Light from outside reflected off the brass case inside the chamber. The street was empty, but lights inside the apartment buildings on this side burned bright. No doubt the police were on the way in response to the gunfire. They had minutes. *Seconds.*

"I want her alive," Chistau added.

Bjerre frowned as he put the gun away. It was a dumb order. He said into the radio, "Why? There is no need for a hostage."

"We need to know how she tracked us."

Bjerre said, "Ask Rayel."

"He's dead. One of the CIA people shot him. Look, I see her now. Third alley down from you."

Bjerre eased the car forward. There! The woman looked smaller half a block away, but he saw the top of her head. She darted from the alley and ducked into a storefront.

She had an automatic weapon.

How the heck was he supposed to take her alive?

Chistau answered the unspoken question.

"Bjerre, me and you converge on the front, the others from behind. We'll box her in. Go, now!"

TRACY CROUCHED in the alcove and braced her weapon into her right shoulder. A car came screeching to a halt on her right. The man behind the wheel opened fire with a handgun. The storefront glass shattered around her, raining down. Tracy tried to cover her eyes with one hand while firing. She rolled out of the way, onto the sidewalk, the bits of fallen glass cutting her exposed skin. She tried to get to her knees; the glass sliced through her pants and into her skin. She tried using her hands. The sharp pieces of broken glass sliced her palms. She screamed. Tracy gained her feet as the man in the car exited. She tried to stand, then felt another bullet nick the back of her left elbow. She flattened and rolled over, the blood on her hands making a positive grip on the Galil impossible. A second car, from the left, stopped short of the parked vehicles curbside, the driver stepping out to cover her with his pistol.

The driver of the second car shouted, "I want her alive!"

Then the gunmen from the alley emerged onto the sidewalk and swarmed around her. She looked left, right, frantic for a way out. There was none. They had her. Parked vehicles blocked her, gun muzzles pointed at her, held by steady hands, while her own bleeding hands couldn't hold her weapon...

One of the gunners stepped forward and smashed the stock of his rifle into the back of her head.

A BUMP in the road jolted the car enough to bring Tracy back from unconsciousness. It wasn't an improvement. Her head hurt from the impact of the gun stock and her face hurt after landing on the sidewalk. Everything else hurt too. She was too big for the trunk, so they'd forced her into a sort-of fetal position. What limbs weren't asleep ached and cramped. They'd zip-tied her arms behind her, so a bigger ache occupied her back, shoulders, and neck.

And it was dark and smelly in the trunk. The only glow came from the emergency release handle on the underside of the trunk lid, which did her no good with her arms behind her back. She had to lie there and hurt until they let her out. Where were they going? She wondered if they were heading for the location pinpointed on Rayel's map. Tracy focused on the moments following their arrival. She'd have more information then and could plan her next move. Even if her next move was to wait until she wasn't sore anymore before making a bigger move.

The man in charge told his men he wanted her alive. Why? His reasoning could provide an advantage later. What good was a hostage to them? The CIA wouldn't give them anything in exchange—they'd leave her hanging. *Sorry, hon, we all know the risks. It's the spy business.*

Another bump. The trunk jolted. Tracy cried out and didn't care if anybody in the car heard. The bump made her hurt all over once again.

A sharp turn. Tracy sensed a left, but then the road

became bumpy again. Constant, despite the car slowing. Tracy didn't stop the yelps and cries. They were off the pavement, and she hoped they were also close to their destination.

GORM BJERRE FOLLOWED Chistau off the paved road and up a two-lane dirt path leading up. Heavy brush and forest were on either side of the dirt road. They were a stone's throw from Merkala Brach in the northern part of the city. From the top of the hill, they could see the Strait of Gibraltar, but not the rock itself.

Chistau's brake lights flared. Bjerre removed his foot from the accelerator to slow as well. He heard the woman's discomfort in the trunk. He didn't appreciate Chistau's insistence they take her. There wasn't anything she knew they didn't have other ways of learning. But Chistau was the boss. He had his own boss issuing the orders. Bjerre needed to argue with the top man, but good luck getting to him. Their group gave a new meaning to "staying within the shadows." No cells knew where the others were or what they were doing. If any faced capture or died in battle, they wouldn't lead authorities to the rest. Only the top man knew the whole story. But it resulted in unexplained orders and Gorm Bjerre wondering what the point was.

Chistau began to speed up. Bjerre pressed on the gas. They were almost to the top. A quick look in the rearview showed the other cars with the surviving gunmen following behind him. Bjerre glanced at the dashboard clock. They had to hurry. The sellers of the nuclear triggers weren't far away. They had maybe thirty minutes.

4

Finally, Bjerre followed Chistau's car through a tight right turn. They passed through the iron gate of their hillside hideout. The gate opened automatically from pressure sensors in the ground. It swung forward, clearing the way. The tall wall around the hideout was solid concrete. Bjerre would have preferred anti-personnel measures on the wall. But it wasn't a military installation. It was a rental. The grounds consisted of thick grass and palm trees. Security lights cast their beams throughout, creating dark shadows around the property. The white two-story stucco house, in the center of the property, loomed large in the shadows.

Thirty minutes. Bjerre shut his car off and hurried out, leaving the driver's door open. He heard Chistau yelling his name, but he ignored the calls. He instead unlocked the trunk and lifted the lid. The woman looked at him with tired eyes, squinting against a glare behind him. He pulled her legs out, then helped shield her head as she rolled out and dropped onto the ground with a grunt. He helped her to her knees, where she caught her breath, and then Chistau came over and kicked her in the back. The wind brushing the palm trees carried away her scream. She landed on her face and shifted and tried to rise again.

"Why are you helping her?" Chistau demanded.

Bjerre said nothing. The two other cars containing their surviving gunners stopped behind him. The shooters exited the cars. Chistau told them to carry their hostage inside. Chistau pulled Bjerre back as the gunmen lifted Tracy off the ground. Two propped her between them, and they headed up the stone path to the house.

Chistau glared at Bjerre, then turned and followed the others. Bjerre shook his head. Enemy or not, there was no reason to behave like animals. They were supposed to be better than the enemy they fought, otherwise the people they fought *for* wouldn't embrace them as their heroes.

But it was typical of revolutionaries, Bjerre decided. Some got the point more than others.

TRACY FELT life coming back to her limbs, the pins-and-needles crawling up her legs at a fast rate. The gunners ushered her along a lighted hall with white walls and decent carpet. *They must have rented in a swanky Airbnb*, she thought. Through a doorway into a spare bedroom, they dropped her on the carpet. She rolled onto her side. The hallway light showed on the grim faces of the gunmen. They didn't look at her with fondness; each one wanted to shoot her over their dead comrades. *You might get your chance soon.* Unless she created an escape plan—and fast.

Two gunners stayed while the others departed. They stood outside the still-open bedroom door. She noticed they all spoke French. But Tracy didn't spot any who looked French. They were a mix of Europeans, and somebody decided French was going to be their common language. *Who decided?*

They kept the room's lights off, but Tracy wasn't interested in where she was. Not yet. She doubted there was anything within the room worthy of a weapon. She knew better than to dismiss the idea outright though. She'd find a useful item if one existed. But with her hands behind her back...

The zip ties at her wrists dug into her skin. It hurt; she'd have preferred the numbness remain. The pain made her start thinking of how to get out of there. Getting her hands in front of her would be a good first move.

Heavy footsteps on the hallway carpet made her pause. A figure stepped into the doorway and gazed at her for a moment. The man who'd kicked her, who'd ordered her taken alive. He was tall with thick black hair and a pock-marked face. Acne scars? She held his gaze. Might as well have a staring contest to show who was the real tough nut.

"You killed six of my men," he said.

"You killed every single one of mine," Tracy said. "Call it even?"

The man entered the room and kicked at Tracy's booted left foot. "Why are your ankles not tied?"

"It's only our first date, honey. Let's not get too carried away."

"Thank you for shooting Rayel. Saved me the trouble."

"Nobody likes a snitch."

"And we are going to shoot you," the man said, "but I need to know some things."

Tracy waited.

"Did Rayel come to you, or did you come looking for somebody vulnerable you could exploit?"

"Good girls don't reveal their secrets, hon."

"We'll torture you before we use a bullet."

"Joke's on you, I'm into that."

"All right, another tactic. You tell me what I want to know, and I make it quick, and right here." The man reached behind his back for a pistol.

Tracy watched him hold the gun in his right hand, clasping his right wrist with his left hand. He looked thoughtful. "Well?"

She said, "Why is this important?"

The man laughed. "Why do you think?"

"Because if we recruited Rayel, his death solves your leak. If he came to us, you have a bigger problem. If he talked, so will another of your crew, like the two bugfucks in the hallway."

"This only ends one way," the man said. "I promised to make it quick, but maybe we'll throw something worse into the mix."

"I hope you soundproofed these walls," she said. "I'm a screamer."

Before the man with the scarred face replied, another figure stepped into the room. The one who'd tried to help her out of the trunk. He tapped the other man on the shoulder, who turned with a frown. "What?"

"They're here."

Tracy's interrogator cursed and turned back to her. His face remained stoic. He put away his gun and followed the other man out. He told the two guards to stay in place.

Tracy let out a breath. Now she needed to try to escape. Her mission was already a failure and there wasn't any way to salvage it; *they're here* only meant one thing. The sellers with the trigger circuits had pressed the doorbell. But all wasn't lost—she'd seen two faces. The CIA would be a step closer to identifying this group if she got back to HQ and put a sketch artist to work.

SAM RAVEN SCALED the wall and dropped over the side. He landed in the dark, in a portion of the yard not covered by the security lights. He remained crouched for a moment, catching his breath, letting his heartbeat settle, scanning the area for threats. He saw none.

Then he was on the move.

Raven's shadow raced across the tips of the thick grass, and he ran hard to keep pace. His heavy pack slowed him more than he would have liked. The extra weight almost made him fall wrong after scaling the outer wall. But he needed the gear. The white stucco house sat in the center of the walled estate, draped in shadow from crisscrossing security lights. The palm trees, their tops swaying in the nighttime breeze, offered plenty of cover. He stopped near a trio of palms, their trunks entwined, creating a solid wall. Stretching out on his belly, he let his eyes and ears do the work. He watched and listened and waited.

He waited in the proverbial "too quiet" and didn't like the silence. His entry had gone without a hitch, unnoticed; he reached the refuge of the trees with ease. Lights burned inside the house; four cars sat in the driveway, one with the trunk open. But the scene wasn't right. What were the buyers doing inside? There should have been guards *outside*. When you're handing over two million US dollars in exchange for a briefcase of nuclear parts, you make sure the trading ground has security.

But silence covered the grounds like a drape. Only the wind and rustling palms made any noise. Sweat from his forehead soaked into the bandanna tied around his head. One thing he knew. He'd beat the buyers to the house. Their vehicles weren't among the parked cars out front.

Raven wore head-to-toe black, including black grease paint on his face. The grease felt heavy and slick. The skintight black tracksuit he wore was fireproof but not bulletproof. He wore body armor under the suit for added protection. His usual weapons adorned the combat webbing across his chest and around his waist. A suppressed autoloading pistol rode on his right hip to deal with sentries. The pistol remained snug in its holster because there were no sentries. His gut told him he'd need the heavier artillery in his pack, and very soon indeed. The pack held the other tools of his lethal trade.

Carefully and quietly, while maintaining a visual scan of the surroundings, Raven slipped the pack from his back and opened the zipper. He withdrew an automatic carbine with a magazine locked in place. The Colt M-4 Commando was a formidable weapon. A short-barreled version of the larger M-4, the Commando retained the larger weapon's ease of use and hard punch. Spare magazines lined his belt on his left hip. No suppressor attached to the barrel. When Raven needed the M-4 Commando, it meant the fight was going hot in a big way. There'd be no need to keep the shooting quiet. The pack contained another weapon made by Heckler & Koch, the M-320 Grenade Launch Module. It was a single-shot weapon capable of firing 40mm grenades and fit onto the holster on his left hip. A bandolier of 40mm shells rode cross-body on his chest. He had a variety of shells to choose from. High explosive, smoke, buckshot, incendiary. The incendiary was good for burning structures to the ground.

He put the pack on again and cinched the straps to tighten it against his body. He grabbed the Colt carbine, flicked the firing selector to full-auto, and watched the front gate. He may have beaten the sellers of the trigger circuits, but they weren't so far behind he'd be waiting much longer.

He hadn't brought night-vision equipment because of the brightness of the security lights, but he wished he had a way to see into the shadows. The biggest threats always concealed themselves in shadows.

Like he did now.

And then a beam of headlights flashed on the front gate.

The sellers had arrived.

5

CHISTAU TOOK THE LEAD AS HE AND BJERRE ADVANCED ALONG the hall to the entryway. It was a large open floor, with a staircase leading to the second floor. A couple of rooms were on the opposite side of the stairs, separated from the staircase by a wall. The owners of the Airbnb decorated it with paintings and mounted sculptures. None of those items occupied Chistau's present attention. He stopped and yelled for his shooters. The men not guarding the woman prisoner ran in from another hallway. Chistau began issuing orders.

"They're here," he told them, echoing Bjerre's words to him. "I want two of you out back and the rest with me out front."

Two gunners ran back the way they'd arrived. The four remaining, and Bjerre, went out to the front porch with Chistau.

Chistau stood under the bright porch light as his four gunmen spread out around the front. The night breeze cooled the sweat on his face and neck. He wasn't done with the prisoner. But for now, he had to focus on the buy. He turned to Bjerre, glanced at the man's empty hands, and snapped, "Where's the money?"

Bjerre choked on his reply.

"Get the money."

Bjerre hurried back inside.

Chistau faced forward again. Headlight beams lit the front gate. The pressure censor in the ground activated the mechanism to swing both sides open. The large Land Rover pulled in and began a slow drive to the house.

I shouldn't have thrown everyone off, Chistau thought. *We're acting like amateurs. We know better. I'm supposed to know better.*

But the boss wanted a few questions answered and Chistau had to provide the answers. This was Chistau's first mission, a major mission, after eight months of training. His men were equally green. None of them were over twenty-six years old. They'd been hand-picked for the job, and their leader expected results. Chistau did not want to return without the prize. The revolution depended on their victory.

Bjerre came back with two heavy briefcases. Chistau sighed with relief.

The Land Rover came closer.

TRACY WANTED to know what was happening outside. The two gunners still stood in the hallway, though. There was no way for her to do anything to free herself. She had to lay on the carpet and be patient.

She had a debt to her team. She couldn't fail.

But what options did she have? The gang would have all the time in the world to deal with her once the sale finished. She needed time, and didn't have any.

Then she had an idea. Carefully, she began scooting deeper into the room, into the shadows. A little bit of cover would help her get her hands in front of her, and then she'd have a chance.

RAVEN WATCHED THE LAND ROVER. He wondered how many rode inside. The porch activity was blocked from view at his present angle, so he moved. Staying flat and low crawling over the grass, he remained in a dark patch not covered by the security lights. Four gunmen. Two waiting at the front door. They were the buyers. He had no idea who they were. Yet. He'd been in Tangier for forty-eight hours tracking the sellers. He knew who the sellers were. He wanted to find out who was buying. And stop them from leaving Tangier with the nuclear parts.

For him, it was another night in his war without end, and he was a man made for war. Sam Raven was a man with a complicated past and an uncertain future. Once he'd worn the uniform of the 82nd Airborne and 5th Special Forces Group. Later, he traded his officer patch for the anonymity of the CIA's Ground Branch.

Raven saw the worst the world had to offer and escaped for a quiet civilian life. But fate dealt a cruel blow with sudden tragedy, and vengeance became his new mission. Now he was freelance. No uniform. No home. Always on the move. The only link to his past was the sterling silver locket around his neck. He never talked about what was inside, but it motivated his crusade. He pursued the world's predators, who created victims and heartache, to deliver justice one bullet at a time.

The Land Rover's brakes squealed as the big SUV stopped. The driver had pulled past the line of parked sedans to get close to the porch. Raven watched the two men near the front door. One held two briefcases—the payment. Raven was too far away to identify their features. But the buyers had covered their tracks well. None of Raven's intel told anything about who they were, or where they'd come from.

He thought of the grenade launcher on his left hip. A couple of high-explosive projectiles would burn them all. But he needed information, too. And he had to recover the triggers intact. Plenty of tasks on the to-do list. He had to do them all the hard way.

The Land Rover's engine remained running. All four doors opened. Six men emerged. Four of them carried submachine guns strapped across their chests. The gunners spread out much like the guards in front of the house. Raven watched and waited. The sellers weren't important tonight. He knew where to find them later. It made sense to let the transaction finish, let the sellers go, and then make his move.

The driver of the Land Rover stopped by the vehicle's front grill. The man who'd exited the passenger side approached the porch. He stopped prior to the steps.

His face was familiar to Raven. He was a German named Felix Wagner. He spoke with a deep voice and Raven heard him clearly when he began speaking to the buyers.

CHISTAU SMILED AT WAGNER, but the stoic German didn't return the expression. Wagner wore black, which did more to highlight his slicked-back blond hair and wire-rimmed glasses than give him an aura of menace.

"Nice house," the German said.

"Got it cheap," Chistau replied. "But we aren't here to discuss my rental agreement."

"Let's see the money."

Chistau gestured to Bjerre, who set both cases flat atop

the porch and popped the locks. He raised each lid. The bright porch light revealed the American dollars packed within each.

Wagner approached to examine the cash. He lifted out several banded packets, flipping through them, confirming it was all real money. Chistau didn't interrupt. When Wagner put the money back, he nodded, then whistled to the man standing before the Rover. The driver moved to the back door, opened it, and reached inside. He removed a large black case, placed it next to Wagner and stepped back.

The outside of the case was wrapped in thick black leather, with buckled straps holding the top closed. Wagner removed the straps with ease and opened the top. Inside, what appeared to be simple PC boards sat in padded slots. Chistau smiled again. Mission almost accomplished.

"You've earned your money," Chistau said.

The stone face returned as Wagner shut both briefcases and picked them up, one in each hand. He nodded to Chistau and returned to the Rover. Wagner, his driver, and the four gunmen climbed aboard and shut the doors. The driver made a U-turn. This time, he drove with more speed to the gate. Within thirty seconds, the Rover passed through and was gone.

"All right," Chistau said. He needed no further command. Bjerre went for the case and carried it inside. The gunners followed. Chistau was the last man in the house, and he secured the dead bolt and lock.

"We leave in thirty minutes," he told them.

Bjerre said, "We're supposed to leave—"

Chistau cut him off with a hard look. "We have unfinished business down the hall. It won't take long."

Chistau started for the hallway. He ignored Bjerre's doubtful face.

TRACY HEARD THE FOOTSTEPS.

She'd worked her zip-tied hands under her bottom and was in the process of pulling her knees closer to her chest to get around her feet, but she stopped. *Dammit.* She'd heard the leader say thirty minutes. She faced a dead end and wasn't kidding herself about her chances of getting away.

She froze, lying still, her mind paralyzed. Sweat beaded on her forehead, dripping down her face. She was outnumbered with no weapon, facing a bunch of men who might take longer than thirty minutes if they were having a good time.

Think, girl, think!

THE CLOCK WAS TICKING, and Raven had to hurry.

He ran for the line of parked sedans. The car with the open trunk was his goal. The raised lid would provide extra cover. Gravel crunched beneath his feet as he left the grass for the pavement. He kneeled behind the car and reached for the H&K grenade launcher.

He saw spots on the ground. They didn't belong. Neither did the large smear on the bumper of the car. He used a pen flash from another pocket for a closer look. Blood. No doubt. From whom? Did they have a prisoner inside?

Raven put the thin flash away and grabbed the grenade launcher. The M-320 was a single-shot breechloader, and he tipped the barrel down to expose the large round chamber. Feeding a 40mm high explosive round into the gap, he snapped it closed and leaned around the car. He aimed for the front door and squeezed the trigger. The M-320 popped as the round discharged. He was firing from short range, but it didn't matter. The tip of the 40mm struck the door and exploded with a violent orange flash and loud boom.

Raven reloaded, this time using an incendiary cartridge from his bandolier. He fired again. The grenade crashed through a front window. The sound of the glass shattering was drowned out by the blast. The incendiary round exploded inside, starting a blaze right away. The fire would engulf the front of the house in seconds and cut off any escape from that direction.

Raven holstered the launcher. From a pouch behind his right hip, he grabbed a gas mask and secured it to his face. The strap around his head pulled the mask tightly to his skin. But he could breathe, and the mask would protect him from suffering the mayhem he planned to unleash in the house.

He gripped the M-4 Commando in both hands and ran to the back of the house as fast as he could. This time, he didn't care if the beams of the security lights found him.

The fight was on.

And he intended to win.

6

CHISTAU ENTERED THE BEDROOM AND FLICKED THE LIGHT switch. The woman, on the floor, averted her eyes from the sudden glare.

"Throw her on the bed," Chistau ordered. The two guards shouldered their weapons and moved toward Tracy. She opened her eyes, but she didn't look at them. She watched Chistau undo his belt, pull it free of the loops around the waistband of his pants, and grin at her.

A few flashes across the face with the buckle end of the belt might loosen her lips and make her talk. If they ran out of time with no answers, no idea how she learned about the sale, then a bullet would silence her forever. And the boss would have to be mad. He'd be less mad knowing they brought back the trigger circuits. There was no need to risk the rest of the mission because of the woman's stubbornness.

The gunners lifted Tracy from the floor. One held her under the arms, the other her legs under the knees. She tried to kick, but the gunner holding on had a good grip. She didn't faze him. They tossed her on the double bed, and she bounced.

Chistau folded the belt and smacked the buckle into the palm of his left hand.

"Feel like talking, or—"

Chistau never finished the question.

An explosion shook the house. The walls rocked with the blast. Chistau and his gunmen froze a moment. Then the team leader hurried to get his belt back on, missing loops, cursing, moving as fast as he could. The woman laughed at his clumsiness. It was a deep, mocking laugh. He wanted to hit her. But they were under attack.

"Protect the package!" he yelled. He ran out of the room and the gunmen followed.

They made it halfway down the hall before the second projectile smashed through a window. The second explosion wasn't as violent as the first, but the blast ignited a fire. The flames spread across the entryway to the walls. Thick smoke and intense heat filled the hallway.

"Keep going!" Chistau urged. Like a real leader, he stayed in front of his men. If he were leading them into hell, he'd get there first.

THE BACK PATIO had the usual furniture. Tables with umbrellas, a barbecue grill. Hedges standing in long brick planters bordered the cement. The planters stood a couple of feet high. Raven dropped to his belly once again and crawled along the left planter. He wanted to reach the hedge facing the patio doors. When he did, he grabbed the grenade launcher once again and slipped a buckshot round into the breech. He fired at the glass doors. The cartridge punched a jagged hole in the glass and exploded inside. The blast sent a cluster of steel balls in all directions. The balls tore through furniture, scarring the walls. If any human bodies were in the way, the steel balls ripped a lot of holes in them.

He loaded another high explosive round and fired again. The explosion in the room beyond the glass filled the room with momentary bright flame. The force of the blast shattered the glass, and shards spread across the patio in a large puddle. Raven loaded another buckshot round, then holstered the launcher. With the M-4 Commando in hand, he started to rise.

More glass broke to the left of the destroyed patio doors. The kitchen windows. Gunmen poked rifle muzzles through the holes. Raven dropped. Two strings of auto fire smacked into the hedge and the brick planter. The slugs zipping overhead or whining off the brick. Raven crawled forward. He reached the corner. He fired back with the Colt carbine, careful full-auto bursts. The windows shattered and pieces fell. Raven shifted to draw the H&K once more. He sent the buckshot round through one of the windows, and the kitchen erupted in flame. A sharp scream within the concussion told him nobody was walking out of the kitchen under his own power.

Raven shoved the launcher into its holster. He ran across the patio and slipped through the empty frame of one of the patio doors. Kitchen to the left, what remained of it. A hallway led to the front of the house, but heavy smoke already filled the passage. A gunman emerged from the smoke, trying to find a target with his rifle. Raven pulled the trigger again and the man dropped. Raven advanced, staying low. A man shouted from down the hallway. Raven had a hard time making out the words, but whoever was talking was for sure the man in charge.

Another automatic rifle blazed to life. Raven ducked back. The rounds chewed into the hallway wall and passed into the kitchen. Raven fired around the corner, blindly, then bolted to cut through the kitchen. He stepped over debris and bodies. Two bodies, mangled, bloody. He had to be careful not to slip. Passing through a doorway into a dining room, he cut right. Smoke filled the sitting room, and he dodged around couches and chairs to reach the room off the blazing entryway. The incendiary charge continued to wreak havoc. The flames ate at the walls and the stairs, creating a thick wall of relentless smoke. The gas mask kept the smoke from choking him or stinging his eyes, but the narrow plastic frame in front of his eyes was less than ideal. It cut off his peripheral vision. Nothing was perfect. But the black tracksuit repelled the flames. Raven stepped through and angled left to the hallway again, the opposite end. Three men clustered there, coughing, yelling, trying to find a way to fight or escape and discovering they were trapped. No way out front or back and they didn't know what to do. A gunner spotted Raven, but died with a bullet through the head before he lifted his weapon. The other two also fell to Raven's salvo, their bodies jerking with the hits. The M-4 locked open, empty, and Raven shoved in another mag and closed the bolt. The bodies weren't moving. There was no need to resume shooting.

Now he needed to find the triggers and get away.

He started forward, but stopped when he heard a woman screaming.

———————

THE BED WAS a big improvement over the floor, but otherwise Tracy's situation hadn't changed. She was very aware of the fact.

The explosions continued. The terrorist gang fussed and yelled as they tried to figure out what to do. They were too young to be seasoned professionals, and it showed as the crisis deepened. Shooting started. Strings of automatic fire and single shots. Tracy began to breathe fast as her pulse quickened. Was this good for her, or worse?

She waited and listened to the continued fighting. One last flurry of rapid shooting, and then the gunfire stopped.

Tracy made up her mind.

She started screaming.

"Help! Help! Don't leave me here!"

She repeated the cries, hoping to break through the sound of the flames and the sensory loss of combat.

She caught her breath for a moment and waited.

Then a large figure dressed in black wearing a gas mask appeared in the doorway. He carried a rifle and other gear. He stared at her, and Tracy began to wonder if she should have instead kept her mouth shut.

———

RAVEN CUT through the smoke in the hallway to the sound of the yelling. He paused in the doorway. A woman was on the bed, hands tied behind her back. The bloody cuts on her skin explained the blood he found outside. She watched him. He examined her. A shock of recognition hit him. He knew this woman! Her hair was darker than when they'd last seen each other, but there was no mistaking the face and fiery eyes of Tracy Donahue. Raven stepped into the room and pulled off his gas mask.

"Tracy?"

"Who the hell are you?"

"Sam Raven."

"Hard to tell with all that crap on your face." But her eyes widened as she remembered. "What the hell are you doing here?"

"The same as you, but not getting tied up. Let's get you out of here."

Raven used a knife to cut the zip tie. She swung off the bed and stood, Raven grabbing her as she almost fell. She held onto him too.

"Lousy place to meet again," she said.

"Where are the triggers?"

"The runt has the case. The second in command, I think."

"Great," Raven said. He had to go back down the hall. "The window is big enough for us to get through." He handed her his knife. "Cut the screen out, and I'll be with you in a moment."

"But the air coming in—"

"There's no other way out, Tracy."

"You have to blow up everything, don't you?"

"It usually works in my favor."

"And *this* time?"

"Maybe I rushed."

Raven donned the mask again and went out. He found the bodies where they fell and spotted the black case. He had to remove the dead man's hand from the handle and bent the fingers back without difficulty. He hauled the case back to the bedroom. Tracy had the window open and was slicing out the screen when Raven shut the door. She swung her legs out and dropped to the ground outside. Raven passed the case through to her, then jumped out too.

"You got a vehicle?" she asked.

"Follow me."

They started running and left the blazing house behind.

7

THEY FOUND KEYS IN ONE OF THE SEDANS PARKED OUT FRONT, so they hopped into the car. Raven tore across the grass to the gate and they waited for it to open. After driving through, Raven stopped on the side of the access road where he and Tracy jumped out. He led her through thick forest to a back road where he'd parked his car, and they drove off again. The big German four-door was quiet and comfortable after the chaos of the house. But the violence still echoed.

Tracy rolled down her window and inhaled the fresh air. Raven was glad for the rush of cold air, too.

"Were you alone?" he asked.

"No," she told him. She went into detail about her mission and how it fell apart and how she lost her team.

"I'm sorry," he said.

"If those sons of bitches had given us our backup—"

"What are you going to do now?"

"Depends on you, Raven."

"Meaning?"

"Are you keeping the triggers, or am I?"

"Take them. Bring it back to the CIA and cut them into poker chips, for all I care. I was just here to make sure it didn't leave Tangier."

"As usual, you seem to be a step ahead of everybody else. How did you find out about it?"

"Usual sources."

"Fine, don't tell me."

"You know how I work, Tracy."

"Yes, I do. Well, thank you. I didn't think I was going to make it out."

"Glad I could be there," he said.

Raven and Tracy first met during a mission in Ukraine. Their partnership wasn't official, but both had personal reasons for being involved. They defeated a false flag operation meant to trigger Moscow's fury and dealt with the betrayal of a mutual friend. Raven wished they could have stopped the Russians altogether, but he wasn't Superman. He could only do so much before greater forces overpowered even his persistent efforts. Such was the problem of a war without end. There never was an end. There were always other victims who needed a champion.

"Do you have a phone?" she asked. "I need to check in."

"Glove box."

She opened it and took out the cell phone stashed within. He gave her the code to unlock it, and she tapped the screen with force as she dialed the number she needed. Raven followed the curving road as it joined with the main and then headed for Merkala Beach. It was a short ride back to the city from there. He listened to Tracy identify herself to her handler and explain the update. Her tone turned defeated as she related the story. She ended with the recovery of the trigger circuits and appearance of Raven. When she ended the call, he asked, "Who's your handler?"

"Evan Graham."

"I don't know him."

"He's been around a while. He wants to know how you got here."

"Tracking the sellers," he said. "My sources pointed to them moving the trigger circuits, but not to whom."

"Did you let them go?"

"Yes."

"Why?"

"Because they're easy to find. I've been on their tail for the last forty-eight hours."

"They'll leave Tangier!"

"I said don't worry about it, Tracy."

"You don't know what you're messing with here, Raven."

"I'm not sure you do, either."

"Part of my assignment was finding out who the buyers were. Nobody knows. Maybe we can identify the bodies and find a clue through them."

"What did you notice when they took you into the house?"

"They were all young," she said. "If any of those guys have reached thirty years of age, I'll buy you a steak dinner. They all spoke French, but nobody spoke it like a native."

"They were also inexperienced," Raven said.

"There must be more to it. This was a new squad, maybe. I can't believe we're facing a terrorist group made up of green peas who are going to freak out anytime you come along with your bombs."

"They knew enough to ambush you and your team."

"True," she said. "But when you set the house on fire—"

"You can train for anything except a no-win situation."

He drove without speaking for a few minutes. They were the only car on the road at the late hour.

He said, "You mentioned something about not having backup?"

"There was supposed to be another team to help us, yes," she said. "But the embassy pulled them back and wanted us to come in as well. Before we could, the ambush started."

"You didn't say anything to your handler about that."

"Now it's my turn to tell you to shut up, Raven."

"I didn't tell you to shut up."

"I'll do my job, you do yours, whatever it is."

"I'm not the enemy, Tracy."

"Stop talking!" she yelled, then fell silent.

Raven didn't chase the topic further. More than the events of the night were bothering her, had her handler added a new piece of information she didn't share? Raven set the thoughts aside. He'd accomplished what he set out to do, but now he had the CIA to deal with. He *always* had the CIA to deal with, it seemed. Most of the trouble he dealt with involved threats to the western world, and they made a good team, when they cooperated. Now and then, the CIA didn't want him around, which only made him work harder. Their resistance often meant an agenda he didn't approve of, posing a risk to the people he was trying to save.

Tracy shifted in her seat. He remained quiet. She was one of the tougher female operatives he'd come across, and helped prevent disaster in Ukraine—until the Russians went in for real. At least their efforts brought Ukraine a couple of extra months, for what little good it did.

"My team is dead and I'm the only one who made it," she said.

"I get it," he told her. "I've lost people. More than I care to admit." *Or think about.* But there were moments when he was alone with his thoughts, where the ghosts of battles past came back to him. He knew their faces, their names. He'd never forget.

"The only reason I survived was because of you."

"Uh-huh."

"I guess I owe you one," she said.

"Whoever we tangled with tonight won't stop," he said, "so you're right. You'll get a chance to pay me back."

8

RAVEN REACHED THE TANGIER CITY LIMITS AND SLOWED THE car. They weren't the only car on the road now, but other vehicles were few and far between.

"Where do you want me to take you?" Raven asked.

"We were at a safehouse. I guess take me there." She used the map feature on his cell phone to plot the way.

"I want you to drop me off a few blocks before," she added.

"Fine." Raven didn't argue. He wasn't an active field officer any longer. He had friends at CIA, but his non-official status did not grant him any favors. Secret houses were secret houses. He followed the directions of the GPS voice on the phone and pulled over when she told him.

"Pop the trunk for me," she said.

He pressed a button under the dash. The trunk lid raised with a *thunk*. He saw the top edge of the lid in the rearview mirror.

Tracy opened her door and put one leg out, then stopped and turned to Raven.

"Guess I'll be seeing you."

"Yeah."

She exited the car and retrieved the black case from the trunk. Raven watched her start walking. He stayed parked until she was out of sight. The move wasn't very smart, but nobody had followed them back to the city. Finally, when he saw her no longer, Raven made a U-turn and headed for his own place of refuge, an out-of-the-way rooming house. He had alcohol wipes to get the grease paint off his face, and a long coat to cover his clothes and rig.

Tracy was feeling the effects of the night's chaos, but when he saw her next, he hoped their bond resurfaced. They'd cheated death in Ukraine, too...together. She told him about her missing father, a military intelligence officer. She was looking for him. He'd vanished after a mission in the Middle East. Zero trace. It was as if he never existed. But she knew he was out there somewhere; or, at least, the truth about his fate was. She wanted to find the truth. Raven had offered to help, but she turned him down.

Maybe they didn't have the connection he thought.

Raven exhaled in an attempt to loosen the tension from his body. He turned his mind to what to do when the sun rose. First priority, get with his sources and tell them to watch the local authorities. When details on the bodies left at the Airbnb came through official channels, he wanted to know.

ENERGY DEPARTED Tracy's body as she walked, but she pressed on. The sudden wave of exhaustion washed over her with expected results. She had a hard time keeping her eyes open.

Shaking her head back and forth as fast as she could, she pulled together. Presently, she reached the town house serving at her team's domicile for the duration of their visit. She knocked on the door with a knuckle, unable to access to electronic lock. Her handler, Evan Graham, had phoned ahead. The house guards were expecting her. When the locks snapped back, the man behind the door confirmed her identity with questions arranged by Graham. Night shift. Only two men on duty. The guard let her inside. His partner wasn't far from the door, and both were armed. Neither asked her where the rest of her team was. She didn't stop to tell them anything or even get water or use the bathroom. She went straight to her bedroom, set the case of nuclear triggers in a corner, and fell on the bed.

Tracy took a few deep breaths. She wanted to cry but nothing came out. After watching the ceiling for a while, she finally visited the bathroom. After a splash of water on her face, she went and found one of the secure phones in the kitchen. She sat at the counter and called Graham.

"I'm back."

"I've been pacing the room waiting for you to call," he said. "We have our people in the Moroccan secret service to get up to speed on this. You have the triggers?"

"I do," she said. "The only thing at the house are bodies, and I'm sure the fire has charred them to the point you'll need their teeth for ID."

"The local authorities are there now, and I'm told it's quite a disaster scene. How did one man do all that?"

"Ask around," Tracy said. "You'll find out how Raven works very quickly."

"All right. Stand down till further notice. Don't leave the safe house. When we know more about what happened and who was there, I'll bring you in."

"Okay."

Her voice faded a little. She had trouble keeping her eyes open.

"Get some rest."

"If I can."

"Try."

"Evan."

"Yes?"

"What about the other thing?"

"Not now. Let me handle it. Go to bed."

She hung up the phone and trudged back to her room. She didn't see the house guards. She didn't care where they were hiding. They were ninjas. Always there, but unseen till needed. She passed the doorways of the bedrooms used by her team. The belongings of dead men surrounded her. Items once possessed with the energy of their owners now sat discarded like deadwood. She didn't want to examine anything. She'd feel like she was violating their trust. Only one thing mattered right now. Bed. She locked her bedroom door and flopped on the mattress once again. There was no point in getting her clothes off.

The night's failure weighed on her for more than one reason. The failure reminded her of another she had to contend with, one always with her, and the associated memories loomed large in her mind as she tried to relax.

Her father. Still missing, presumed dead now, and still no answers. She at least had answers to bring home regarding her team. The widows, children, and significant others would have the closure, or at least the sanctioned closure, she never received. Did her father die, anonymously, somewhere too? And would there ever be any trace of where he'd been?

Graham's orders to stay put took her attention next. Graham was going to send her home. She had no doubt. The Agency wanted to keep her there till the situation stabilized, and then they'd put her on a plane back to the US.

As she dozed, as the thoughts shuffled through, she caught scent of the smoke on her clothes and skin. She felt the pain of the cuts received during the ambush. She was back there again, trapped, panicking as exhaustion took over; then there was only Raven, decked out in black with a mask over his face, coming through the doorway to carry her to safety.

Someday, he wouldn't be there when she needed him. Tracy didn't want to think of the choices she'd face when that day arrived. She wondered if it was best to get out of field work, or the CIA altogether, while she remained in one piece.

Finally, she slept. No nightmares disturbed her.

9

RAVEN PARKED ON THE STREET OUTSIDE THE ROOMING HOUSE. It was a small, nondescript building blending with all the others along the street. The ground floor was a convenience store, the rooms making up the four floors above. He used several alcohol wipes to clean his face, but still felt the greasy residue on his skin. Then he removed his chest rig and combat belt. He moved awkwardly in the confines of the car, but released both items and put them in a tote bag. The rig and belt joined his weapons already within, and he zipped the bag shut. Leaving the car, he donned a long tan overcoat. The edge of the flap went to his calves. He didn't expect to run into anybody, but he wasn't going to walk in carrying his weapons either.

He used a key at a door beside the store, entering into a narrow stairwell. The walls and steps showed plenty of age, but the place was clean and the landlady took cash without asking questions. Raven locked the door behind him and took the steps to the fourth floor. A second key unlocked his room. He stood in the small room a moment and let himself adjust to the quiet.

It would have been nice to have a team of his own on this mission, but he felt better working alone. He only called for help when there was no other option. So far, he was doing fine by himself. He didn't want to feel responsible when a teammate fell in battle. It had happened more than he wanted to admit already, as he'd told Tracy. More than he wanted to admit, indeed.

Raven lived by two rules. The first was not getting involved in a shooting while in public. Too many innocents might get hurt, and he detested collateral damage. The goal of his crusade was to protect and avenge victims, not create more. He'd avoid a fight if he could, or lead the enemy to a location where a shootout wouldn't pose a risk to civilians.

But sometimes, despite his best efforts, a public fight was inevitable. In those cases, he had to make sure his aim was sure, and the fight didn't last long.

Rule Two: No roots. Raven's home sat on water. He lived on a houseboat at a harbor in Stockholm, Sweden. He wasn't there often. The war without end kept him on the move. Always on the move.

After turning the dead bolt and sliding the chain in place, he set his gear in a corner and stripped off his clothes. The smell of smoke lingered in the fabric. The short shower felt good, and he didn't rush. Next stop, bed. He wanted to call his contact, Oscar Morey, right away. The former gangster turned intel broker wouldn't appreciate a call in the middle of the night, so he didn't. He had only to wait a few hours until sunup. Once the new day arrived, they could address the unanswered questions in detail.

He knew for a fact the buyers would try again. But who were they, where were they, and what did they intend to do with the parts they wanted to collect? How big of a bomb did they intend to build?

Raven put the thoughts away and let sleep claim him.

EVAN GRAHAM of the CIA wondered when he'd get a chance to sleep.

He never seemed to find the end of his responsibilities.

Official or otherwise.

He wasn't at the US Embassy in Rabat overseeing Tracy's operation, but at a hotel in Tangier with a secure connection to his embassy office. He had his reasons for not being with the rest of his colleagues, but the easy excuse was he wanted to be close to his team as they carried out their mission. When he used his personal cell phone to call somebody in the United States, he crossed the line from official to unofficial. But the call was important. The man on the other end of the line needed to know about the failed sale. Most importantly, he needed to know who intervened to cause the problem.

Graham was a career CIA officer but part of the new breed. Long hair tied back, battered jeans, tennis shoes. If he ever wore a suit and tie, it was because he was back at headquarters attending meetings. Boring meetings. Meetings with the top brass who had no idea what sacrifices and decisions field work required. They'd never worked in the field themselves, but thought they knew how he should do his job. They caused more problems than they solved. Graham was happy to be overseas and away from HQ and hoped to be away from HQ for as long as possible.

Graham was slim and wiry. He had enough muscle to prove he was no pushover when a situation required such a demonstration, which wasn't often, because he wasn't an idiot, and he spent most of his time behind a desk. He had the necessary training and practiced often.

He was, however, an opportunist.

Some might use the word *traitor*.

The man at the other end of the phone call answered with a gruff, "What is it?"

"It's Graham."

"Tell me what happened."

"Total screw up."

"Explain."

The voice gave the impression of a middle-aged man who'd achieved enough success he no longer needed to impress anyone. There was nothing more for him to prove. People came to *him* now. People needed *his* approval.

But Harrison Hunt did have something to prove, and Evan Graham was helping him prove it.

Graham said, "Tracy survived."

"The rest of the team?"

"They're dead."

"Will anybody question why you pulled the backup squad?"

"No, because the locals *did* make a fuss. We had to do it."

"How did Tracy get through?"

"They captured her and took her to the house."

"They *what*?"

"She says the team leader wanted to question her about how she found out about the exchange. *His* boss ordered him to do so."

"I trust you will shortly have a talk with *his* boss?"

"He's on my list."

Hunt was in charge of the project, but isolated. Only Graham had his contact information and knew what the field team was doing. Graham was the go-between with the new terrorist cell. The cell wanted to make their mark on the world; helping a billionaire become a private nuclear power would for sure give them a leg up on al-Qaeda or any other six-pack of terrorists one could think of.

Hunt said, "Then what happened?"

"A new player showed up. A man named Sam Raven."

"Is his name supposed to mean something to me?" asked Harrison Hunt.

"He's a freelance. Sort of an international do-gooder who likes sticking his nose where it doesn't belong. Used to be CIA too. Lots of friends. Getting rid of him won't be easy."

"But you have a plan to do so."

Graham blinked as he listened. Hunt hadn't asked a question; he'd stated a fact.

And, luckily, Graham indeed had a plan. He was happy to share his idea.

"Yes, I have a plan in mind. We need to keep Tracy on the case because Raven will stick with her. It will make them both easy targets."

"All right. And the triggers?"

"She has them. I'll get them to you."

"We only need the triggers and our plan can proceed."

"I'm keeping Tracy under wraps for the time being. The components aren't going anywhere."

"Fine. I need to go. Got a guest spot on CNBC I need to make."

Before Graham could say goodbye, Harrison Hunt hung up the phone.

10

TWO MORE CALLS. THE FIRST WOULD BE EASY. OVER AND done. The other? Graham expected he'd be awake for a while longer.

Before making the first of the pair, he brewed another pot of coffee and poured a cup. He was using his official CIA coffee mug. The mug was a rich navy blue with the CIA logo etched on one side. Everybody joked whether the mugs were bugged or not. Nobody wanted to break one to see for sure. If the mug did have a bug, Graham was in deep trouble. But they weren't. He'd have been found out months ago if it were the case.

Sitting at the hotel room table, cluttered with papers and various items, he used his personal cell again.

He was going to wake up a dangerous man with the phone call, but lots of money soothed the savage beast.

Two rings. Graham picked up his coffee.

"I had a feeling you'd be calling."

Graham set down the mug. August Lloyd was always direct and to the point, but his statement startled Graham.

"Why?"

"Lots of rumors last few days. Go ask around. A few of us were expecting fireworks and it looks like tonight somebody touched them off. What's happening?"

Lloyd was a killer for hire. Always available when the CIA wanted to use a large amount of money to make a problem disappear.

"You know I can't give details," Graham said. "But I need your help cleaning things up."

"How many?"

"Two."

"I'll need the usual target package. Decent pictures?"

"You'll have them."

"Deadline?"

"ASAP. But no screw ups and no comebacks."

"You know my methods," Lloyd said.

And Graham did. ASAP could mean six months if Lloyd didn't like the conditions in which he found his targets. He'd wait for the prime opportunity, the one which would allow him to get away without a trace.

"Usual remuneration?" Graham said.

"Fine," Lloyd told him.

Graham wasn't going to mention the job wasn't official, and he knew Lloyd wouldn't ask. Lloyd was a good soldier who assumed the best from his primary US employer. Graham didn't think he'd be too upset even if he knew the truth. But it was best to keep the details hidden. The less who knew what was going on with Harrison Hunt and his personal terrorist cell, the better.

GRAHAM ENDED his call with Lloyd and forwarded the information on Raven and Tracy. He made sure to remove mention of their CIA backgrounds. Lloyd needed to think they were terrorists or criminals or generic bad guys of the week.

One last call.

Graham yawned and poured another cup of coffee. It wasn't helping. He didn't feel awake or sharp. He only felt tired.

The second chat was short.

"He wants to see you," said the woman on the opposite end of the line. She always answered first.

"When?"

"Now."

Graham sighed.

"He won't talk to you over the phone."

"Fine."

"Be outside in ten minutes."

Graham knew better than to be in the presence of Cassiano La Bella without a gun. The man had a temper and liked to yell. His girlfriend, the woman on the phone, knew how to rein him in, however. Graham wore a pistol under his jacket while waiting outside the house. A black Mercedes with tinted windows came around the corner. The bright headlamps flashed over his face. He didn't cover his eyes. The car stopped in front of him, and he opened the passenger door. A woman sat behind the wheel. She was the lady he'd spoken with on the phone. Simona Vadala didn't look as striking in person as she did on her Instagram page, where she posed in photos taken in exotic locations wearing expensive outfits. The public knew her as an international "influencer." Her travels were a good cover for her Marxist activities. She used capitalism as a weapon against...the capitalists. She wanted to toss a hand grenade into the entire system and had no trouble using the system to destroy the system.

Her long dark hair was tied back, and her dark eyes

weren't as prominent in the low light of the car. She wore casual clothes, jeans and a T-shirt, and drove away from the curb as soon as Graham shut his door.

"Cassiano has been up all night," she said.

"Haven't we all?"

"It's not funny. He lost good friends tonight."

"We may have lost everything tonight, Simona."

"Is our sponsor—"

"He's not happy. I'm not happy. And I'm about to make Cassiano even less happy than he is now. What was he thinking asking for a prisoner?"

"He was trying to help."

"We don't need him to help. We need him to do what we pay him to do. You let me worry about what's going on with the Americans."

Simona stopped talking and Graham didn't continue, either. He wasn't going to waste his breath on the team leader's main squeeze. She had nothing to do with his decisions; she was his girlfriend, and a field operator. Yelling at her was only a waste of time.

But he did feel for Cassiano La Bella. It wasn't easy to lose friends in action. Sudden death was a way of life in Graham's line of work. The spy business was like a hungry shark. Everybody had an equal chance of getting devoured, but it depended on where you stood when the jaws snapped shut.

THE DRIVE TOOK TWENTY MINUTES. Simona eased the Mercedes into the garage below a nondescript brick building. She and Cassiano La Bella lived in the top loft. The rest of the building was empty.

She parked the car, and they entered a noisy elevator to get to the loft. Simona used a special key to unlock access to the top before pressing the floor button. The gears and machinery clanked and groaned. Graham would have preferred the stairs, but didn't want to spend energy he didn't have climbing to the top. Most of the floors had no walls closing them off from view of the elevator car. Graham took note of the bare concrete, gray and lifeless, and debris spread across the lower floors. When the elevator stopped at the top loft, the scene changed.

They stepped off the elevator into a well-insulated, furnished front room. The open floor plan stretched ahead to the opposite end of the building, where a wall of glass looked out on the city. Kitchen, living spaces, bedroom divided from the rest by a curtain. It might be a temporary home, but Simona and Cassiano knew how to make the space work.

"He's out on the deck," she said. Simona led Graham through the loft to a sliding glass door on the opposite end. The "deck" wasn't large; a narrow walkway with a rail was a better description. But it was a place on which one could watch the city or the stars and Cassiano La Bella spent a lot of time looking at both. La Bella turned from the city view as Graham stepped onto the steel platform. The look in the eyes of the younger man wasn't inviting. Graham was glad he'd brought his gun.

———

"You want to tell me what happened?" Cassiano La Bella said.

"Do you want to tell me what the hell you were thinking?" Graham countered.

"We won't accomplish anything if you two start fighting," Simona told them.

Cassiano snapped his fingers at Simona. She glared but turned and went back inside.

"She has a point," he admitted.

Graham said nothing for a moment. He knew Cassiano La Bella as a rising star in the New Marxist underground. But those calling themselves "New Marxists" were the same as the old Marxists; the ideology hadn't changed, only the names of its advocates. Graham stood facing a man younger than him, but wealthier, with the kind of family connections Graham would have killed for. Cassiano La Bella had so much of his privileged life handed to him, he now wanted to spread the love to the lesser mortals. Free them from their capitalist oppression or some shit. Graham cared little for the ideology. What he cared more for was money and power, and Harrison Hunt offered both. The New Marxists were a means to Hunt's end, but La Bella and his crew didn't understand their position in the pecking order.

Most of the New Marxists were content to only preach and publish and find teaching positions at universities. Spread the gospel without violence. Get enough people on their side, people who demanded the changes required, and reach their utopian goals without firing a shot. Cassiano La Bella was not one of them. He wanted to usher in the revolution using a gun. Meet the New Terrorists, same as the Old Terrorists. The goals never changed. Only the faces.

"A lot of my friends died tonight," Cassiano said. "I want to know why."

"I only know a little of what happened," the CIA man said.

"Tell me. Please."

He's remembering his place, Graham thought. "The sellers had somebody watching them. A man named Sam Raven." Graham related the story, once again, based on Tracy's narrative. "And the only reason I know this, Cassiano, is because you made the horrible decision to take prisoners."

"We had to find out how the CIA found out. *You* certainly were no help."

"Watch it, kid."

"I'm serious. You should have told us a team was in-country with orders to stop the sale. You didn't find out—"

"I knew from the beginning."

"And you said *nothing*?" Cassiano immediately lowered his voice. A tap on the window. Simona wagged a finger at him. He glared at her. To Graham, "Explain."

"You know how easy it is to blow my cover? Some things gotta play out, Cass. I tipped the locals and they put on the pressure to get the backup team removed and then your people did the rest. We were almost home free, and then you had a brain fart. Now we have *two* loose ends. I can control one, but not the other."

"How did they find out? I need to know how they found out!"

"Why?"

"This is my mission as much as yours. I have honor and pride on the line. I've made a lot of promises—"

"And you don't want anybody to think you can't keep them."

"Yes."

Graham nodded. "Rayel got nervous and talked. That's it, Cass. There's nothing else to it. He got word to the right people, and they sent the team. We'd have been fine to whack the unit and Rayel, but you asked for prisoners."

"You're going to blame this on me?"

"No," Graham said. "From a strategic point, I appreciate the effort. If it were any other operation, you'd have done the right thing. But you have to have confidence in me on my end, or this isn't going to work and our sponsor is going to cut loose. Get it?"

"What do we do now?"

"You don't need to worry about my end. Worry about your own."

Cassiano frowned. "You mean the council."

"I mean the council, yes. The authorities will identify the bodies of your compatriots and start asking questions. They'll end up at the council's front door."

"I'll tell them Chistau and Bjerre and the others were working alone. I'll tell them I tried to stop them but failed."

"Will they believe you?"

"They'll believe my father's donation money."

Graham chuckled without humor. Rich kids always escaped accountability as soon as they waved Daddy's money around.

"What about this man named Raven?" Cassiano asked.

"I'm taking care of it."

"I want a piece."

"You're too exposed as it is. Let my people handle it."

"How am I supposed to get experience—"

"You gonna pull the trigger yourself?"

"At least let my people act as scouts."

Graham considered the idea a moment. "I'll talk to my guy. Maybe we can work that out." *Gotta give somewhere. Kid wants to redeem himself.*

"If your man fails, you can use my people."

"I don't expect him to fail."

"Problems happen."

"They do."

Cassiano La Bella told Simona to stay put. He wanted to drive Graham home. She didn't reply. Graham noted she looked indifferent.

11

When Cassiano returned, he found Simona half asleep in bed. He sat on the edge of the bed beside her. She opened her eyes as his weight sank onto the mattress.

"Get some sleep," she said.

"How? This mission was supposed to make me a star."

"I thought this mission was supposed to advance our cause." She was awake now and sat up against the headboard. The headboard bumped the wall. She wore her blue flannel pajamas. Nothing sexy about them. Her hair hung lazily down her shoulders. Without makeup, she looked plain. Simply another young woman in a sea of same. She didn't look like an Instagram star in the middle of the night.

She added, "What is this *me* garbage, Cass?"

"You know what I mean."

"I'm afraid I don't. Are you in this for you, or the rest of us?"

"For us. Of course," he stressed. "But what I mean is…to be associated with such a coup, to get the parts we needed for the bomb. Nobody's ever done it before, Simona. *Nobody.* Do you understand how huge this will be?"

"You want to be the world's next greatest revolutionary leader, is that it?"

"I've told you this."

"But you have the rest of us to consider. This isn't about your ego."

"I know."

"So why are you talking out of your ass?"

"Because we're failing!" Cassiano didn't shout but hissed the last word with venom. He stood and began to pace in front of the curtained windows. "Now what do we do? Now what?" He put his hands on his hips and turned to face the woman in bed. He stopped pacing.

"We try again," she said.

Cassiano let the words sink into his mind. He didn't reply right away.

"Once we get rid of Sam Raven and the other woman," Simona continued, "our path will be clear. Even with Graham's assassin on the job, we should watch them ourselves."

"How do we find them?"

"If we spread out and look, it shouldn't be too hard. Did you discuss it further with Graham in the car?"

"I tried to convince him."

"Did you?"

"I don't think so," Cassiano said. "He thinks we're better off laying low until he solves the problem."

"He has as much at stake as we do, Cass," she said.

"I'll be to bed in a while," he said, and left the room. He shut the door behind him. Heading for the kitchen, he found a bottle of vodka and poured a small shot into a glass. He wasn't getting to sleep without help. He sat at the table by the large windows overlooking the city and his face was sour.

He'd been born to wealth and privilege. His father owned several companies and pulled in millions of dollars in profit over the years. He had everything growing up but saw too many people with nothing. Never mind the middle class, those who had enough, but never as much as they wanted; it was those living in poverty he lacked the ability to erase from his mind. Why should his family have everything while others had nothing? And why did his father think it was wrong to want to give them some of the excess? Because they hadn't earned it? They had trouble enough—why punish them further? Pass some of the gravy along. What was the problem?

Cassiano's attitude carried on through college where he met a group of like-minded students. They attended lectures from a professor named Ernesto Montego. He was from Latin America but taught throughout Europe. On the side, he ran the Council of Economic Equality. The job of the council was to assist governments in identifying those in the most need and tending to them. Montego's inspiring words fired up Cassiano's activism further. Cassiano found himself in class less and less and more and more under Montego's private tutelage. Montego had a past, however, he didn't like to talk about. He'd once been a violent radical, part of a group called Z-11. He and his brothers and sisters in arms tore a path of violence and destruction throughout Latin America to bring about the socialist ideal, but it came at too high a price. Montego lost friends; almost died himself; spent ten years in prison. He swore upon release to only preach and publish. Teach the ideal. Bring about change through peaceful means. But Cassiano found himself inspired as much by Montego's words and his previous actions. It was in the action where Cassiano found his true calling. He wasn't content to talk. He wanted to fight the bastards who kept the rest of society in chains, who didn't care who suffered so long as they had their luxury.

Cassiano and some of his fellow students began talking

on their own. Planning. Engaging in what-if sessions. Reading books by and about radicals. Discussing the lives of previous revolutionaries. One of Montego's assistants overheard them and made a few suggestions. Cassiano and his fellows soon found themselves in the desert, somewhere in the Middle East, where older men who knew the ins and outs of combat trained them. The classes were more intense than anything they found at university. How to use small arms. Build explosives. How to kill up close. When they returned to Europe, they had orders to sit and wait and carry on with their lives as if they'd never left. But very soon, Evan Graham arrived and made a proposition impossible to refuse.

Graham claimed to represent "a sponsor" who needed a job done. A simple job collecting parts. Parts for what? Never mind. A few on Cassiano's crew figured it out, though. Parts for a bomb. And not a regular bomb, a big one. A nuke. Their job was to collect the key components, the trigger circuits. A nuke couldn't detonate without precise timing. The trigger circuits controlled the timing. If any step in the detonation process suffered a delay, the nuke wouldn't go off. It wouldn't destroy. And destruction was the goal. Destruction of the old order; the rising of a new one from the ashes.

But they'd failed. They didn't get the circuits. Chistau and Bjerre were dead, as were several others he'd come to look at as brothers. Family. Real family. Now they were dead.

Now he understood why Montego pursued peace instead of war.

But aggression won out. He wanted revenge. He wanted to get his hands on Sam Raven and the CIA woman and tear them to pieces. Scatter the bits to dogs. He wanted to do the same to anybody else who tried to get in his way. He'd kill Graham too if the CIA traitor forced his hand, but only after getting the name of "the sponsor" out of him.

Cassiano finished the glass and placed it in the sink, the spotless sink. Simona couldn't tolerate anything out of place or dirty. But he left it in the sink anyway. She'd holler at him in the morning. At least, by then, he'd have had some sleep.

Back in the bedroom, he took off his clothes and climbed in next to Simona's warm body. She was already snoring. He must have been more tired than he realized. He expected to stare at her or the ceiling for a while. He didn't. Soon he was snoring too.

12

Tracy had coffee ready by the time Graham arrived at the safehouse. She knew the first words out of his mouth would be, "Any coffee ready?" and she wasn't wrong. The safe house guards answered the door and let the CIA handler inside; Tracy met him in the hall. He followed her to the kitchen.

"Did you manage to sleep?" he asked. It was his second question. He sat on a stool at the kitchen counter.

"More than I expected," Tracy replied. She poured his coffee into a plain white mug and set it on the counter. She had already set out a selection of creamers and he absently examined each. He did so to avoid Tracy's icy stare.

Graham finally popped open two creamers and dumped the contents into his coffee. Then he met Tracy's eyes.

Tracy had neglected to set an alarm for when she wanted to get out of bed. The foul stench from her clothes and body finally forced her awake and into the shower. She spent forty-five minutes under the hot spray. After putting on clean clothes and tying back her hair, she cooked more than she could eat for breakfast. The guards helped finish what she didn't get to. Last, she placed the briefcase containing the nuclear triggers on the dining table. The table sat behind Graham's spot at the kitchen counter. If he noticed, he'd so far given no sign.

"Tell me what's on your mind, Tracy."

"Oh, you're gonna hear what's on my mind, all right."

Graham sipped from his mug and waited.

"How did the locals get involved, and why do you think somebody betrayed us?"

"Somebody knew. Somebody tipped off the other side. Who else but a traitor?"

"I killed the informant because I thought he set us up."

"See?"

"No, I don't, Evan. Why take a prisoner if Rayel cracked and told them about us? They asked me basic questions. They didn't know *anything*."

"Then we need to look inside our own house," Graham said.

"Which puts everything on hold and me on a plane for home, right?"

"You're not going home yet. Stuff with the buyers is on hold till we identify the bodies. In the meantime, I want you to look into the sellers. How did they get the triggers?"

Tracy's face remained stoic.

"What's the matter?"

"Me staying here goes against protocol," she said. "What about my debrief? I should be off the case because of how close I am to the guys who died."

Graham raised an eyebrow. "Do you truly feel like following protocol right now, Tracy?"

"No."

"Good. Neither do I."

"But, Graham—"

"I argued against the usual process. Bought us a couple of

days. A couple of *days*, Tracy. We don't have much time. Do you think Raven will help?"

"I can ask."

"Where is he?"

"I have no idea," she said.

"Can you get a hold of him?"

"Why is the CIA so concerned with Sam Raven?"

"The CIA isn't concerned at all. I am. I'm asking for myself. If we only have a couple of days, we might as well put everything we can on the playing field."

"Raven doesn't work for free."

"We'll figure out an arrangement, don't worry. Can you reach him?"

"No," she said.

Graham sighed with frustration. "Well, any ideas how to find him then?"

Tracy scoffed. "Maybe the other side can try to kill me again. Raven showed up the last time they tried."

"At the last second."

"You sound disappointed he didn't wait longer."

Graham shook his head and drank some more coffee. "Come on, Tracy. You know that isn't true. The only reason I'm asking about Raven is because you told me he'd tracked the sellers. Seems to make sense we'd ask him to share what he knows about them, right?"

"Sure."

"See what you can do." Graham scooted off the counter stool.

"I'll go outside and yell his name," she said. "He should come running."

Graham finally acknowledged the briefcase sitting on the dining table. "Are the triggers in this case?"

"They're all yours, Evan."

Graham picked up the case. "We have a NEST crew

coming for these. They'll be back in the US and in a lab in less than twenty-four hours. We need to know where they came from."

"Blame the Russians. Everybody else does."

Graham laughed without humor and Tracy escorted him to the door. One of the two guards unlocked the door for Graham to exit. Neither he nor Tracy said goodbye to one another. The silence hung thick between them until the guard closed the door.

GRAHAM RETURNED TO HIS CAR. He set the briefcase in the back seat. He thought it was funny to be carrying nuclear weapon parts in the back of a government-issue sedan. Nobody would believe the story. He'd never be able to utter a single word about the situation anyway.

He drove away and thought about the conversation. The best part about the chat was the coffee. Either Tracy knew how to brew a mean cup, or the CIA, for once, splurged and stocked a safe house with the good stuff.

He'd feel so much better if Tracy had died with the others, but they'd still have a mess to clean up. Raven still would have shown up at the worst possible time. But he wouldn't have a very smart woman doubting every word he said in a safe house kitchen over a cup of coffee. He'd only have one person to kill instead of two, and nobody would lose any sleep over the death of Sam Raven. Tracy was right about one thing. What happened to her team would get the full investigative treatment, and soon. He had to get the deal done with before then.

But the triggers were going to NEST. He'd no longer have control over the components.

NEST was the Nuclear Emergency Support Team, part of

the Department of Energy. The trigger circuits in the back seat of the car were for use only in a nuclear bomb. Collecting the parts and taking them back to the US fell under NEST's responsibility. It created a problem for Graham, however. He'd promised to bring the triggers to Harrison Hunt. Now he had no way of delivering, which added another problem to solve...

13

TRACY WASN'T SURE IF INSTINCT OR PARANOIA KEPT HER FROM telling Graham the truth, but didn't want to dwell on the question too long. She wasn't positive on the answer, and should she reach a conclusion, she didn't want to process the implications. She had no loyalty to Graham. They hadn't met until she and her team arrived in Tangier. He was the in-country contact, nothing more. She wanted to find out how the op went bad. She owed it to her team to be sure of the answers. It wasn't helpful to chase paranoid suppositions or questionable instincts.

But she hadn't given her true answer on the "can you reach Raven?" question. Of course she could. She didn't call from the safe house, though. She cleaned up in the kitchen and went to her bedroom for a pistol, a Glock-19 9mm she'd carried for several years. Then she let the guards know she was going out for fresh air and hit the street. She wore the handgun on her right hip and let her untucked shirt cover the weapon.

It was a quiet afternoon. A light breeze made the palm

trees lining the roadway sway. There was a lot of activity at a sports complex on the opposite judging by the full parking lot. The large building didn't offer any clues, but the adjacent tennis court had plenty of players. She fought the urge to stop and watch. She'd played tennis in college but hadn't stayed with the sport. She continued walking. At the end of the neighborhood, open dirt lots created space between the mass of residential buildings. She jogged through, the level of the ground rising and falling, staying close to the buildings on her right. When she reached the next street, she slowed to a walk and found a bench. She sat and took out her phone.

Raven answered after the third ring.

"You okay, Tracy?"

"My goodness, Raven—"

"What's happening?"

"I don't know."

"Where are you?"

"A block or two from the safe house. How about a ride somewhere?"

"Any place in particular?"

"We'll pick a direction and find something." She gave him the street and cross street and he promised to be there shortly. She put away her phone and listened to the wind for a while.

———————————

RAVEN FOUND her where she said she'd be, but he was driving on the opposite side of the street. He used a roundabout to turn back her way, pulled over, and she climbed into the car.

"Thanks," she said as she fastened her seat belt.

Raven pulled back into the light traffic. "No sweat. You eat anything today?"

"I had a big breakfast, but I won't say no to coffee."

"I know a nice place not far away."

Tangier had a coffee culture to rival Europe and the United States. Cafés, full-service coffee shops, and small street vendors dominated the city. Raven found a café facing a busy intersection and they took a table near the kitchen. It would have been nice to sit up front and watch the street traffic, or they could have watched the construction of a new series of buildings across the street. But Raven didn't want the exposure. He had a feeling Tracy wanted to stay away from the crowd, too. She sat next to him at the table; both of their backs to the wall. Her eyes never stopped scanning the front door and the café in general. She not only looked tired, which he expected, but sadness lingered behind her alert expression. She was relying on combat awareness to mask inner turmoil. He did the same, quite often. It was the only way to shut out emotions until it was safe enough to examine them in turn.

"I'm sorry about your men," he said.

"Me too."

She'd selected a cup of cardamom coffee, a spiced blend popular in the Middle East and India. It had a powerful aroma, which was strong in the café—she wasn't the only one partaking. Raven, never a fan of coffee, selected a green tea with a little milk.

"Why don't you tell me what's going on," he said.

"I'm not sure who I can trust, except you," she began. Tracy filled him in on her conversation with Graham, and how she'd turned the trigger circuits over to him. She told him he wanted Raven's help in finding out how the sellers acquired the circuits. She added Graham brought up the idea of somebody betraying the operation.

"Does he have any proof?" Raven asked.

"He doesn't. He brought it up last night when we were in

the car, and I pressed him on it this morning. We couldn't have been set up by our informant, because the buyers wanted to know how we found out what they were doing."

"How many knew about this operation?"

"The usual suspects at Langley. A couple of CIA people at the embassy in Rabat. Me and my team and Graham."

"Who told the Moroccans?"

"I don't know. Somebody at the embassy. Maybe the leak is on the Moroccan side. But how would they have known all the details? That could only have come from somebody at the embassy."

"Is Graham going to poke around?"

"I didn't ask. I suppose he will."

Raven nodded. "What do you need from me?"

"I guess some help with the sellers. You said you'd been tracking them."

Raven nodded again. He was watching the crowd outside and the people inside, too. A leak meant Tracy remained a target. Graham, too. If the opposition had people still looking for Tracy, they might make a move against her in public. And put innocent people in danger. Raven didn't want to spend any more time at the café than he had to.

"All right," he said, "here's the story. Your analysts are going to find one of the triggers has Soviet origin, and the other is a copy."

"What?"

"At the end of the Cold War, we had a deal with the Soviets to get rid of the buried suitcase nukes. They weren't a myth."

"I'm aware," she said. She drank some coffee.

"But in the process, the team digging up the nukes diverted one elsewhere and dismantled it down to the last part."

"No way," Tracy said. "You can't make one of those disappear. There had to be dozens of eyes on them."

"There weren't," Raven said. "Less than ten people. They wanted to keep the effort as restricted as possible. Nobody could know what was going on."

"A mix of Americans and Russians?"

"Yeah. Each made sure the other did what they'd agreed to. Somebody doctored the inventory to hide the missing bomb, and the only reason we know about this at all—"

"Somebody talked?"

Raven nodded. "Death bed confession. One of the Russians. His co-conspirators took the dismantled parts and began selling them. Their retirement plan. The original trigger wound up in the hands of the sellers we met last night."

"How did they make a copy?"

"It's not hard when you have the real deal as a reference."

"And the rest of the bomb parts?"

"Russians are working on it, and so is the CIA—*quietly.*"

"Guess I wasn't need-to-know."

"Nope. This is locked down tighter than Fort Knox."

"But you're not working for the CIA," she said.

"No. I got a tip and found out the story through my usual sources."

Tracy shook her head. "We have leaks everywhere."

"And some of them aren't bad," he added.

"Where are the sellers now?"

"Still here in Morocco, and laying low until the heat's off, though I'm sure there's a plan to slip away when nobody's watching."

Tracy drank some more coffee. Raven hadn't touched his tea. He tried it—luckily, it hadn't gone cold. But it was getting close. He drank some more.

"Who's in charge of the sellers?" Tracy said.

Raven took his cell phone from inside his jacket and tapped the screen. He pulled up a picture and showed it to Tracy. The photo showed an older man with dark hair. He wore a gray suit and was in the process of getting into a large sedan. His narrow eyes appeared to take in everything around him as he slid into the car, but he never saw the camera focused on him.

"This is the ringleader. A Frenchman named Genest. Roch Genest. His number two was at the house last night. A German named Wagner. Genest has an estate outside the city. Heavily guarded. I'm sure he's beefed up his force since last night, too."

"We should go see him. If they made one copy, they may have more."

"You got an army?"

"Only me."

"Well, two of us ought to be enough." He grinned and put his phone away.

"I don't think it's funny, Raven."

"It isn't, but I'm thinking of how well we worked together in Ukraine."

"I don't want to talk about Ukraine."

"Neither do I." Raven swallowed more tea.

"Whatever we do," she continued, "I'm not telling Graham."

"You think he's the leak?"

"No, but he'll report to somebody, and *that* somebody is the person we can't trust. I hope," she added. She tried to cover her worried expression with another drink. Raven saw through the shield. It was Graham she didn't trust, but couldn't articulate why yet.

"Fair enough," he said.

"We go now?"

"Tracy, you know better than that. We'll go look. See what we're up against. We might *need* an army."

"Hope not," she said.

"I have friends in low places," Raven told her. "If we need help, they aren't far away."

14

RAVEN TOOK THE LEAD AS THEY EXITED THE CAFÉ, BUT TRACY walked behind him with her hand on his shoulder. It wasn't a romantic gesture; she wanted him to know she was there while he shielded her. They made a left turn, the street bathed in shadow. The buildings on either side of the street blocked the sun. Despite the shade, it was still warm. The breeze from the Med, behind them, matched the temperature.

An overpass noisy with traffic flow loomed ahead. Tracy switched to Raven's left and walked beside him. His rental waited curbside not far away. Tracy kept her head "on a swivel," glancing behind them, ahead, one side or the other, looking for threats. She didn't notice where Raven was looking until her second scan. Then she took notice.

"You see the two guys on motorcycles?" she asked.

"I do."

The two riders wore normal street clothes and sat atop dirt bikes with thick tires. Their jackets were too bulky for the weather. They made a show of talking to each other, but their eyes were on Raven and Tracy. They'd been watching Raven's car.

"What do you think?" she asked him.

"We can't get into a shooting match with all these people around."

They reached Raven's car. He unlocked the passenger door and opened it for her. She locked her seat belt in place. Raven dropped behind the wheel and started the car. They were parked with the car's back end facing the pair on the motorcycles. When Raven pulled away from the curb, they headed away from the pair. Tracy turned her head but didn't have to look too hard. Raven told her they were coming after them. She saw the pair merge into traffic.

"Where are we going?" she asked.

"Are you armed?" Raven asked instead.

"Got my Glock and a spare mag."

"One spare?"

"I wasn't expecting a war, Raven."

She faced forward again. The traffic flow wasn't bad. They headed for Oujda Avenue, passing through roundabout to eastbound Mohammed Avenue VI. Raven continued west, and Oujda became Mohammed Avenue. Tracy tried to picture the city map in her head. Raven wanted to get away from innocent bystanders who might be hurt in a crossfire. Mohammed Ave VI traveled east–west along the coast; she had no idea where Raven wanted to go. His flat expression and focus assured her he had a plan; at least, she hoped he had a plan.

She turned in her seat to look back, adjusting the seat belt so it didn't impede her movement. The motorcycle riders remained behind them, several car lengths back. They were using the other cars for cover. How long till they started shooting?

"You got a plan?" She faced forward again.

"We may have to improvise."

Tracy let out a hard breath. "I'd much prefer a plan, Raven."

"Me, too," he said.

RAVEN DIDN'T HAVE SO MUCH as a plan but an idea of what to do should a situation develop. He'd picked the café close to Mohammed Avenue for a reason. If the pizza hit the fan, as it appeared to have, he knew a quick way out of the city to a less populated area. Rule One: no gunfights in public. And he hoped the pair of the motorbikes didn't decide to open fire while on the roadway. Accurate shooting from a moving vehicle wasn't easily accomplished even by experts.

He eased into the left lane and pressed the accelerator. The motorcycles kept up but remained back far enough to show they weren't ready to engage. They were scouts for the crew wagons loaded with gunners who'd do all the shooting. Unless Raven found a way to shake them before the main force arrived.

Coastal water and sand to his left. It was a nice day for such a drive, though his mind wasn't on appreciating the natural beauty of Tangier. Plenty of beach goers were taking advantage, as well, and their lounge spots dotted the sand. Raven's attention remained ahead. They passed through other portions of the city. The urban sprawl was thick, structures stacked against each other. They created the illusion of one big building with many extended side buildings. The road began to incline as it stretched ahead.

Another glance in the rearview mirror. The motorcycles kept their distance but maintained the same pace.

Mohammed Avenue continued through a busy part of town catering to tourists. Multiple hotels overlooked the

Strait of Gibraltar. Traffic thickened for a moment as drivers slowed for exits. By the time Mohammed Avenue became du Front de Mar, they were speeding up and on their way to the N-16 motorway.

"Why didn't cut through there?" she asked.

"Not my plan."

"We could lose them."

"You sure?" he said.

Tracy fell silent. He saw the concern growing on her face. He understood. The motorcyclists were only a prelude. The bigger problem had yet to surface. She for sure did not have the ammunition to engage in a protracted gun fight. Raven's own weapon wasn't a match for a full gun crew, either. He carried his Nighthawk Custom Talon .45 autoloader in his usual shoulder harness. The gun hung under his left arm, while two spare magazines hung under his right. Twenty-four total rounds. Against two gunners on motorcycles, probably enough. Against more? He wasn't sure.

A slowdown through a roundabout; quick turn to continue eastbound; they were on the N-16 and going faster. For a few minutes, the motorcycles faded from view. Raven moved from the left lane to the middle and back again to get around other vehicles, but he kept his speed up. Thick trees replaced urban sprawl. The road inclined upward once again. The trees blocked the view of the water.

"Tell me what we're doing," Tracy said with a raised voice.

Raven checked the rearview again and cursed.

"Talk to me, Raven!"

"They're catching up and now there's another car with them."

A white sedan with blacked-out windows kept pace with the motorcyclists, who rode on either side. They weren't bothering to mix with traffic anymore and occupied the three left lanes. Their formation acted as a rolling block to

give traffic behind them a hard time passing. Other drivers
had to swerve into the right lane to get by. They sped toward
Raven's car.

"Oh, great." Tracy shifted in her seat and grabbed her
pistol from the holster on her right hip. She checked the
Glock-19's chamber and held the gun in her lap.

"Get ready to jump out," Raven said.

"Get ready to *what*?"

Raven moved his right foot from the accelerator to the
brake pedal. A turn lane appeared down the center of the
roadway. He braked, shifted into the turn lane, then
wrenched the wheel left. Oncoming traffic honked; slowed;
tires screeched. By the time he crossed the road and entered
the forest, he'd left behind a backup that blocked access to
the turnoff. Temporarily. But disrupting the enemy for a
short time was better than no time at all.

THE RENTAL ROCKED as it left solid pavement for a dirt path, a
dirt path wide enough for two cars, but still a dirt path. He
quickly steered through a tight right turn. The trees became
denser and blocked the sight of the road. He sped along the
path with a cloud of dust drifting high behind him. Another
turn—left this time. The tires gouged the earth as he spun the
wheel.

Raven followed the path until he found a small cutout in
the trees on his right. He aimed the car for the cutout, slowing, and eased as close to the tree line as possible. He yelled
for Tracy to get out. He was out of the car himself and
running around to her side by the time her feet hit the
ground. He grabbed her left arm and led her into the trees.
They had to dodge around the thick foliage. Ground debris
consisted of hollowed-out tree trunks and overgrowth, along

with dried leaves and dead branches, and hampered their forward movement. The dry leaves crunched and the dead branches snapped as their steps landed, but they powered through. Raven found a fallen trunk of decent size, and they jumped behind it to face the direction of the road again. Tracy breathed harder than Raven. Both slowed to normal by the time the motorcycles arrived. The chugging engines announced their arrival before Raven and Tracy saw them. The bikers stopped and shut off their engines. Dismounting, they approached the parked rental and drew machine pistols from under their bulky jackets.

Then the white sedan arrived next.

Raven estimated they were only twenty yards away. To move further would only cause enough noise for the enemy to spot them. Raven wanted to wait and see what they did next, but he'd yet to take out his gun. Tracy held her Glock in her right fist.

Only one man emerged from the white sedan.

"Can you see his face?" Raven said.

"Not yet," Tracy said.

The man from the sedan wore dark sunglasses. Raven only caught a fleeting glimpse as he checked out the rental. The trio stayed low behind the car to cut off the view from the forest. Raven nudged Tracy. Time to move while the enemy worked out their strategy. He and Tracy moved deeper into the coverage, keeping the crunching noises to a minimum. Ocean waves crashed in the distance. They weren't far from another beach, which meant people, which meant—

Raven grabbed Tracy's arm and they dropped into an overgrown dip and peered over the top. He ignored the edges of leaves and the sharp pokes of twigs and branches trying to cut through his clothing. Insects buzzed around them.

"I can't see the car," Tracy said.

Raven watched rather than spoke. He ran through scenarios in his mind. The man with the sunglasses was in charge. Would he lead his men into a situation where an ambush awaited them? Or—

Crunch. Snap.

Raven spotted the trio working their way through the trees. Their boots landed on dried foliage and announced every other step, same as it had done for Raven and Tracy. The three kept wide gaps between them, not bunching up or staying close. They moved in the practiced manner of military vets. Only the two motorcyclists displayed weapons. The man with the sunglasses had empty hands. And they weren't turning to search in a pattern or splitting up to cover a wider area. They were heading straight through. Straight through—

"To the rear," Raven whispered.

"What?"

"They're trying to circle behind and cut us off."

"What do we do?"

He grinned at her.

RAVEN WAS SWEATING HARD by the time he was close enough to strike.

They didn't have a lot of ground to play in. He and Tracy had to slink through their own route to pick up the trio's trail and close in from the rear. Everybody moved slowly and methodically. Raven and Tracy paused when the enemy paused and moved then they moved. Now Raven was close enough to the rear gunman to start the offensive, and he did so with swift results.

He left cover and ran at the rear man. His heavy footsteps

thumped on the ground, and the man began to turn. Using a fallen branch like a baseball bat, Raven swung at the gunman's head. *Whack*. The man toppled to the forest floor with a loud thud. The noise was loud enough to get his two pals to turn around. When they did, Tracy opened fire with her Glock-19, three rapid shots. Sunglasses and his remaining gunner ducked and rolled as the slugs zeroed on them. Her shots smacked into the brush.

Raven stayed on the ground and grabbed the unconscious man's machine pistol. The weapon was a Brugger & Thomet APC with the stock folded. Raven snapped the stock into position and tucked the weapon into his shoulder. He fired a burst at the back of the second motorcycle rider. The rounds tore into the foliage and then ripped through the bulky jacket. A short cry, and no further movement. Raven moved forward with Tracy moving right, away from him. Now for Sunglasses.

The man in charge poked a pistol through a bush and Raven ducked and rolled as he fired twice. He heard Tracy shooting behind him. Raven rose to a knee and sprayed the bush with another salvo from the machine pistol. They were running out of time; somebody would hear the shots and call the authorities. The machine pistol locked open as the mag emptied. He dropped the B&T and grabbed his pistol. Raven found Sunglasses on his back behind the bush. Blood soaked his clothes; a chunk of his neck was gone. There was no need for a follow-up shot from the handgun. He put the Nighthawk .45 away. Tracy reached him and gasped as Raven removed the sunglasses from the man's eyes.

"You know him?" he asked.

"I know who he is, yes," she told him, breathing hard still.

Raven raced through his pat down of the body, checking pockets, grabbing a wallet, car keys, and a cell phone. He pocketed the wallet and keys and examined the phone. He hoped the phone especially helped lead them to whoever hired the killers—it might explain Tracy's security leak. The screen was locked and required a biometric sweep to open. The dead man's body was still warm, but there was a chance it wouldn't work. The man was dead, after all. But not a lot of time had passed. The body hadn't cooled or gone into rigor. Raven took the chance. He used the man's index finger to touch the screen. The lock warning vanished to reveal the home screen. He then turned off the locking feature, confirmed he could access the list of previous numbers, and put the phone with the other two items. Tracy watched without comment.

"Let's get out of here," he said.

Raven and Tracy hurried back the way they'd come, his clothes wet with sweat, Tracy stomping after him. He had questions, and he hoped she had answers.

15

FROM THE OUTSIDE, RAVEN AND TRACY LOOKED LIKE A COUPLE taking a leisurely afternoon drive. Other motorists paid them no mind as traffic flowed on the N-16 back to the city.

But inside Raven's rental car, the conversation was tense.

"You said you knew him?" Raven asked her.

"I know who he is, we've never met," Tracy explained.

"Tell me."

"His name was Arnold Lloyd. Mean anything to you?"

"No."

"Ex-CIA. He was for hire, still working for CIA but only when he accepted a contract."

"A contract? He was a hitter?"

"Yup."

Raven dug the dead man's cell phone out of the outer pocket of his jacket. He handed it to Tracy and told her to find something useful on it, but the names in the contacts didn't register with her. Some on the list were obvious code names. Other numbers had no name attached. Raven grimaced. He knew people who could run traces on every recent number, but none of them were in Tangier.

"You know anybody you can check those numbers?" he asked.

"I did, yes. He died last night."

Raven let out a frustrated sigh and decided to keep his mouth shut. Tracy placed the captured phone in the center console. Raven still had Oscar Morey and his crew in Greece, and he could read the numbers off to them. But a trace would take time. Raven wasn't sure they had the luxury of waiting, and by the time Oscar found a clue—if one existed—they'd have uncovered other evidence. Holding on to the phone might spook whoever hired Lloyd, however. When the cops found the man's body without his personal items, word would get back to whoever hired him...

Make the traitor nervous and he'll make a mistake. And when he makes a mistake, he'll expose his treachery. There'd be no need to hard proof. The traitor's actions would provide all the proof required.

It wasn't a solid plan, more of a Hail Mary; but Raven had used such tactics before, with varying results. He wasn't sure what else to do for the moment.

Tracy broke the silence. "I don't want to stay at the safehouse."

"What do you have in mind?"

"What do you *think*, Raven? I want to get my stuff and find somewhere else to stay."

"Stay with me. Plenty of room."

"You sure?"

"They're after both of us, Tracy. We'll have a better chance of surviving if we work together."

"Like last time."

"Yeah. And like last time, one of our own is following a personal agenda and getting people killed."

"Or trying to. Arnold Lloyd won't be the only killer they send after us."

Raven drove on.

Tracy took less than five minutes to get her gear together. On the way out, she noticed her team's belongings were gone, already cleaned out. Her men might as well have never set foot in Tangier. The only trace of them lay in the morgue.

She let the house guards know she'd be back in a while, but didn't think they cared very much. Their job was keeping the house secure, not keeping an eye on the people who stayed.

Raven drove to his rooming house and led her up the stairs to his door.

"At least it doesn't smell," she said.

"It's quiet," he added. Unlocking the door, he let her enter first and then turned the locks and hooked the chain.

"Not much bigger than a hotel room," she said.

"It's fine."

"Who gets the couch?"

"I'll take the couch, Tracy, don't worry."

She set her pack on the couch and glanced at the curtained windows. Light filtered through, but not much. Raven turned on lights to brighten the space. She knew better than to ask him to open the curtains. She'd have left them closed, too. Can't risk snipers on the roof across the street. Paranoia. Part of their lives.

Raven crossed to the small and worn kitchen. Nothing looked new, but everything looked clean. From a corner refrigerator, he grabbed two bottles of water. They sat on the couch and she cracked her bottle open and drank half before attempting to speak. Raven only took small sips and waited for her.

"What do you want to know?" she asked. *As if I need to guess.*

"Who might have hired Lloyd?"

"You mean, could Graham have hired Lloyd?"

"Do they know each other?"

She shrugged. "I told you, I didn't meet Graham until we arrived here. I have no idea who he knows and doesn't know, and I doubt we can check his social media to find out."

"You better not reach out to him for now."

"I agree."

Raven drank more of his water and set the bottle on the coffee table. He took out his phone. Tracy put her bottle on the table as well and asked Raven where the bathroom was. He pointed down a dark hallway, and she excused herself. She needed a moment to get away from Raven's glare. She wasn't saying what he wanted her to say. Graham hired Lloyd; Graham was the traitor; Graham betrayed them. She could speculate on other reasons, but the appearance of Lloyd, a freelance CIA employee, pointed at Graham. There was no other reason. And if they could crack Lloyd's cell phone, they'd find the connection they needed.

"Took you long enough to call," said Oscar Morey.

Raven grinned and shifted on the couch. Oscar Morey, former gangster, now served as a conduit of information and intelligence to interested parties—for a price. But he helped Raven free of charge. The pair forged a bond many years earlier.

Oscar Morey hadn't always been on the side of the angels. He was an underworld character, well-known in Europe, but one who managed never to spend a day in jail. With ears to the ground in many areas, and contacts all over the world, there wasn't anything he couldn't discover when given enough time. After many years of using Sweden as a home base, he'd recently relocated to Greece.

Years earlier, when a much younger Raven was in Paris to kill a man responsible for several murders, Morey had intercepted him with a warning. Raven's target was one of Morey's soldiers; he wanted Raven to stay out of his business. *You don't want this kind of trouble.* Raven explained why his target had to die and drew Morey to his side. Some crimes were too heinous for even Morey to tolerate, and he allowed Raven to finish his mission.

Later, after Raven saved one of Oscar's kids from certain death, the underworld legend pledged his support. From there, the bond between them grew. Raven was smart enough to know when fortune handed him a talisman. In this case, a crusty old bastard named Oscar Morey.

"The heat's on," Raven told Oscar, giving him a brief rundown of what had taken place since the opening battle.

"What do you need to know now?"

Raven said, "I need to know what the Moroccan police or secret service is saying about the bodies."

"Way ahead of you. Get this. The dead guys have links to the Marxist underground in Eastern and Western Europe. And they all have one thing in common: a university professor named Ernesto Montego."

"Where does he teach at?"

"Berlin. His background is even richer. He did time for blowing shit up in Latin America. While in prison, he reformed. Now he teaches and publishes and runs an outfit called the Council of Economic Equality. He puts up videos on YouTube now and then if you want to watch him."

"I may have to," Raven said. "What about the names of the dead guys?"

"Nothing will mean anything to you. Gorm Bjerre and

Javier Chistau are two of them; the Moroccans think one or the other was in charge of the team. They haven't even graduated from college yet. No police records of any kind. The only suspicious activity is a two-month alleged vacation in the middle of a semester. Nobody is certain where they went yet."

"A training camp?"

"Probably," Oscar said.

"Well, it didn't do them much good. They were far too green for what they faced." Raven didn't feel sorry for the wanna-be fighters. A fair fight was do-gooder Lone Ranger stuff. A fair fight had no place in the real world. If they wanted to be terrorist killers, they'd die like the other terrorist killers he sent into darkness.

Raven asked, "Who else are they connected to? Friends, associates, classmates. They can't have been working on their own. They were errand boys. A squad sent out for a mission."

"Working on it."

"But the Montego lead..." Raven trailed off a moment and Oscar didn't interrupt. He continued, "Worst case, if we come up dry here, we go to Berlin next."

"Anything else?"

Raven took out the dead killer's cell phone and swiped the screen. "I have a bunch of phone numbers I need traced. I want to know who's on the other end of those numbers. Got a pen?"

"Go."

Raven started reading off the recent numbers, focusing on any calls made from the time he arrived in Tangier. He figured he was going back too far, but wanted the bases covered. He read off the numbers with no names, and the ones with names or code names. It took a few minutes, and Oscar read back each one to make sure he'd written them correctly.

"We'll get on this right away," Oscar said.

"I'm looking specifically for somebody named Evan Graham."

"Got it. You been in touch with CIA yet?"

"The CIA just flushed my toilet, Oscar."

"What?"

Raven laughed and ended the call. He imagined Oscar's perplexed expression and laughed again.

Tracy asked him what was so funny when she returned.

He told her.

16

EVAN GRAHAM HAD TO HIDE HIS DISTASTE FOR THE MAN ON
the computer screen. He hadn't wanted to answer the video
call, but his boss demanded an update. It was better than the
boss ordering him back to headquarters in the US to answer
the questions, though.

Graham didn't like Christopher Fisher, the CIA's Deputy
Director of Operations. The man was old-school, the suit-
and-tie type. Graham, with his longish hair and preference
for street clothes, didn't fit with the spit-and-polish crowd.
He conformed, when necessary, but tried to keep those
moments to a minimum. He knew Fisher didn't care for him,
either. They clashed on more than one occasion because of it.

Fisher let Graham know right away he wasn't happy.

"You've lost control of the situation, Evan."

Graham weighed a response. There was no sense trying
to argue his way out of Fisher's statement. Four men dead
and no leads on the terrorists was for sure a bad state in
which to find his operation.

"I agree," Graham said. "We had all the bad breaks. But at
least we recovered the trigger circuits."

"When does NEST arrive to take custody?"

"I sent the case with the triggers to the embassy this morning. NEST should be in Rabat by now, so they'll be on the way home within a couple of hours."

Graham was still at his hotel in Tangier. He'd called a courier to bring the case to the embassy as soon as he'd returned from seeing Tracy at the safehouse. He'd have to explain to Harrison Hunt why he'd failed to keep possession of them. The truth was, the longer he held onto them, the more he risked exposing his role in the deal. He had to avoid suspicion at all costs. The stress of playing both sides hadn't broken him yet, but he felt the pressure over every inch of his body. And his mind. Sudden aches and pains. Scattered thoughts. A sense of disorientation at random moments. He was on the verge of making a fatal mistake if he wasn't careful.

Fisher continued. "Getting the triggers back is fine, but we still have problems. You've heard about Arnold Lloyd?"

Graham blinked. *Hold your poker face...*

"We got the alert after the police found the body, yes."

"I want to know what he was doing there. Was he on a job for us?"

"No."

"When the local government finds out he was one of us—"

"I'm aware of the potential blowback, Chris."

"You're saying you have no idea why he was there?"

"None at all. He must have been working for somebody else."

"Not his style."

"Well, money—"

"Lloyd wasn't motivated by money; he was motivated by service to his country. We can't exactly call around and find out who was paying his bill, even if he was working for a friendly government."

Graham didn't respond. *What can I say?*

All he knew was he had to also explain to Harrison Hunt why his plan to get rid of Sam Raven and Tracy Donahue went up in smoke. And left three dead behind.

"Considering the situation," Fisher said further, "Lloyd doesn't fit the puzzle, and I don't like it."

"He had his support network," Graham said. "We can get in touch with them."

"But we can't guarantee they'll give us anything."

"Him being killed might loosen their lips, Chris."

"All right, try it. I need answers, Evan. I expect you'll have them when we talk again in forty-eight hours."

"Okay."

Fisher blinked off.

Graham closed the laptop and put his face in his hands. His exhale carried weight he wanted to get rid of, but next he had to call Harrison Hunt and have an even tougher conversation.

———————————

THE LITTLE APARTMENT wasn't big enough for two, but Raven and Tracy tried not to collide too often. As he sat on the couch with a notebook and pen, he scribbled an action plan. Looking at his words and running the scenario through his head, he decided it was good enough. Tracy fussed in the kitchen while he worked. When he arrived in Tangier, Raven stocked the small refrigerator with fresh meat and chicken and vegetables. Tracy removed items from the refrigerator while muttering under her breath about recipe ideas. Raven was a basic cook; she knew more, so Tracy offered to make dinner. They were both starving.

Raven made a few corrections to his idea and the desired result of the action. It seemed okay but plans never survive first contact with the enemy. At that point, plans were only an idea to keep in mind. A goal to reach. Steps to take. The rest? Make it up as you go along, son. He used his cell to call a number in the United States. The number connected to a CIA officer who worked at headquarters. Clark Wilson, Senior Staff Operations Officer for the CIA's Special Activities Center, was one of Raven's contacts at the Agency. And an old friend.

Clark sounded irritated when he answered. His curt, "Yes?" gave Raven the impulse to get straight to business.

"It's Sam. Got some time?"

"For you, yes," Clark said. His tone changed to one of relief. "I just got out of a meeting with Fisher. Your name came up. What are you doing in Tangier?"

"I see Evan Graham is keeping his reports up to date."

"He's on the short list for a posting in the smallest corner of the world at the rate he's going."

"It might be worse than that, Clark."

"Start from the beginning."

Raven gave the rundown on his mission to Tangier, and his current whereabouts with Tracy. When he mentioned the assassin named Arnold Lloyd, Clark jumped into the conversation.

"Lloyd is one of the reasons Fisher's popped a gasket. He was one of us. Graham had no idea why he was there, and neither did any of our people at the embassy. And you shot him dead?"

"Him or me, Clark, I didn't stop to ask for names."

"Jesus, Sam—"

"Graham may have hired him. Out of his own pocket. Or somebody else's."

"Can you prove it?"

"Working on it right now," Raven said. "We recovered Lloyd's phone, and I have my people tracing recent numbers. One might be Graham's."

"I'm glad this isn't my operation."

"But you're still in the thick of it."

"Rank has its disadvantages, too."

"Even if we come up with nothing on those phone numbers, I have an idea we can use to flush Graham out."

"Go on."

"The group who sold the nuke triggers made a copy from the original. They reverse engineered them." Raven explained who the sellers were, and what they did with the bomb parts. "They may have a stockpile by now. Which means—"

"Does the other side know this?"

"I can't be sure. I'm assuming they don't."

"It's a big assumption."

"They'd have made a move, and we likely would have seen the fireworks."

"All right, what's your plan?"

"Update Graham's report. Claim my info on Genest and the sellers came from a confidential informant. He'll see it. If he tells his buddies—"

"They'll go looking for another pair."

"We'll have them all in one place."

"I don't have enough aspirin for the headache this will cause."

"Bad apples are like the poor, Clark. They'll always be with us."

"You're a warrior and a philosopher, Sam."

———

RAVEN ENDED the call and joined Tracy in the kitchen. She

was dicing a raw chicken breast with rice boiling in a pot on the stove.

"What can I help with?"

"Grab that other knife," she said, "and start chopping vegetables. I'm doing a stir fry over rice."

Raven began chopping celery and carrots. He worked fast. The tapping blade made a rhythm on the cutting board.

"What did Clark say?"

He told her.

"So, for now," she said, "we're waiting for your friend Oscar?"

"Correct." Raven scooped the piles of chopped carrot and celery into a bowl.

"The sooner he gets back to us, the better. We need to be sure."

"We'll be sure." Raven continued chopping. He didn't tell her of the alternative he had in mind, of going to Graham and dangling him over the edge of a roof until he confessed.

He didn't think it was time for such a drastic move.

"Slow down," Tracy said. "You're going to cut your fingers off."

Raven laughed. "Old habit. Get it done quick and move on."

"Like the rest of your life?"

He paused and looked at the knife in his hand and the results of his cutting. "Sure." He continued, going slower this time.

She touched his arm. "I didn't mean to—"

"You didn't."

"Are you sure?"

"I tell myself all the time we need a rest."

"Who's *we*?"

He smiled without showing his teeth, but his eyes were sad. "Me, myself, everybody."

Raven grabbed another pair of celery sticks and went to work. Tracy went back to her task. She wasn't wrong. He always hurried from one thing to the next, chasing the war, never stopping long enough to catch his breath. When he did, it was to fight off exhaustion. It wasn't any way to live, but he'd made his decisions long ago, alone, over a pair of graves, and saw no end in sight. What Tracy didn't see was the sterling silver locket around his neck and under his shirt. He never talked about what was in it, but what was inside motivated his fight. The ghosts of battles past urged him on, kept him alive, and only when they were satisfied would the war end.

Raven finished chopping and Tracy said she'd take it from there. He went back to the couch and sat quietly.

Tracy made an excellent meal.

OSCAR MOREY CALLED after they finished eating. He confirmed one of the phone numbers on Arnold Lloyd's cell connected with Evan Graham's *personal* phone, not his Agency device. Raven and Tracy listened on the speaker as they sat at the small dining table, the remains of her very good stir fry spread before them. Raven took the news without a reaction, but Tracy's color changed. Raven decided she'd hoped for a different answer. Granted, so had he, but the pitfalls of the spy business gave no quarter. Sometimes, the enemy was closer than you realized.

Raven updated Clark Wilson, who also didn't appreciate the news. He promised to update Graham's file as discussed. Raven wanted Graham to take the bait. He didn't want to have to go to plan B.

"WHAT IS HE GOING TO DO?"

Evan Graham considered the question as he paced the hotel room. Part of his mind was focused on the conversation, the other half thinking of the room as a prison cell. And the walls were closing in by the moment. He spoke with Harrison Hunt on his cell.

"Worst case, I'll be recalled and replaced. They'll send a team out to investigate every move me and Tracy Donahue have made since we started the mission."

"Then we need to move fast," Harrison Hunt said. "Very fast, indeed."

"I drafted a plan to hijack the triggers from the NEST team."

"Do you think La Bella and his people are up to such a task?"

"They'll face six armed men and an armored vehicle. I think they can pull it off, but it's the timing. We only have a couple of hours."

"Not good enough," Hunt said. "If we rush, we fail. Another source is our best bet."

"You can't simply buy a nuclear trigger at Walmart, Harrison."

"You aren't thinking in three dimensions, Evan."

Graham was going to reply, and had his mouth open to do so, when his laptop dinged. A notification. The computer sat on a table against the wall. The table was cluttered with folders and papers and a cup of cold coffee. He told Hunt to hang on a moment instead. The notification window in the bottom right corner referenced his Tangier report. Graham clicked on the window and opened the notification. A note advised of additional information added to the report. Graham accessed the file and jumped to the last page, where the addendum had been added by SSOO Clark Wilson at HQ.

"We just got a break," Graham said. He read the note to Hunt. A confidential informant communicated with Agency officers at the embassy in Rabat. The informant mentioned the sellers of the nuclear triggers by name, and said they'd duplicated the parts to sell to more than one client. The informant advised other triggers existed, and the CIA should intercept the sellers.

Harrison Hunt went quiet after Graham read the notation. Then he said: "Far too convenient, wouldn't you say?"

"It makes sense, though."

"Why?"

"There were two triggers in the case. If only *one* of the suitcase nukes existed—"

"I see your point."

Graham sat in front of the laptop and waited. His pulse quickened with excitement. If the sellers had more triggers…

"Do we know where these sellers are?" Hunt asked.

Graham scanned the note, but a location for where to find Genest and his people did not appear.

"No," he told Hunt. "But La Bella made the original arrangement. He can contact them again."

"We're done talking. Get with La Bella. Have him make another deal. But Graham? I think you need extra help."

"What do you suggest?"

"I'll send you somebody. We'll work out a code arrangement so you know I sent him. I'll get back to you."

"One man?"

"He's all you're going to need. Trust me."

Graham's sixth sense told him not to.

But he said, "Okay," and the conversation concluded.

17

IT WAS TIME FOR A NIGHT OUT.

Roch Genest, French arms dealer, liked a good party. He wasn't as young as he used to be and found his age and appearance made him less attractive to women. For him, younger women liking older men was a myth. He could still put the booze away and ogle young women, and it was almost as good because he didn't have to spend any money on them. Besides, he'd had enough female action in his life to know there was nothing the younger ladies could teach him. He figured it was best to enjoy himself and leave the lothario spirit in the past where it belonged.

He brought his number two, Felix Wagner, with him to his preferred nightclub in downtown Tangier. The city embraced its nightlife in a big way, and some of the best nightclubs in the world called Tangier home. Genest liked a club called Triple 8, where he could have a private sitting area above the dance floor. The VIP section included a pair of dedicated wait staff who knew how to take care of high rollers such as himself.

The drive to the club in his chauffeured Mercedes was

not without business talk, however. Genest and Wagner needed to figure out what to do with the young hot head named Cassiano La Bella. He'd called Genest to make a second attempt at buying nuclear triggers. He even offered to double what he paid last time. Genest told him no. Cassiano went into a tirade. Genest hung up the phone.

"He's more trouble than he's worth," Genest said.

He and Wagner sat beside each other in the back seat. Where Wagner was lean and tall, Genest was the opposite. He appeared thin from behind, but from the front, his expanding belly took center stage. His shirts fit tight over his belly, threatening to burst the buttons, but he refused to get larger shirts. He liked the tighter fit because, despite the appearance of being out of shape, he had nothing to hide. He was confident enough to present himself as-is with no apologies. As a bonus, he found his attitude often intimidated those seeking his services. Nobody knew what to do with somebody who had nothing to hide about himself. It made them less confident to see his confidence. Genest embraced the dynamic and used it to his advantage.

He wasn't afraid to fight, either. Genest was a veteran of the French Foreign Legion and knew how to handle himself. He'd admit he wasn't in "fighting shape" but also knew he could vindicate himself should a situation ever turn ugly.

"From now on," Genest continued, "we don't deal with anybody under forty."

Wagner stifled a laugh. "I'll ask them their age first thing."

"It will be amusing, for sure."

"I want to know who he's working for," Wagner said. "He's not doing this with his own funding. Somebody is using him as a smokescreen."

"It's a good question," Genest agreed. "If we have time later, we should devote resources to finding out. The information will be worth something."

Genest knew the details would also be nice to keep in his back pocket, as a bargaining chip, in case he was ever arrested.

The Frenchman and the German had been in the business of selling illegal arms for the better part of a decade. They'd never dealt with equipment as dangerous as nuclear bomb parts. Offering such items for sale brought out the wrong type of people. People like Cassiano La Bella, who was quick with a pile of cash but too hot tempered to take seriously.

The chauffeur slowed as they approached the Triple 8 and stopped out front. A long line to the door stretched along the sidewalk and extended half a block. The bright signs announced the name of the club and joined the other bright lights and signs along the street. The area wasn't lit up like daytime, but it was close. Traffic was thick and noisy. Genest and Wagner didn't bother with the line. They exited the car and presented cards to the doorman, who let them through. They had the upper deck of the club reserved. Genest and Wagner received curious glances as they went inside, but they ignored them. A few more heads turned their way when they entered, and they ignored those too.

But they should have paid attention to two faces in particular.

RAVEN KNEW he'd catch Roch Genest at the Triple 8. Just like he had when he'd first arrived in Tangier.

He and Tracy were both dressed to blend in with the club's clientele. Raven wore black, with a leather jacket covering his pistol. Tracy's blue party dress and long hair made sure nobody spent too much time looking at Raven. They occupied a small table on a raised platform close to the dance floor. A gold rail separated the platform from the dance floor. Tables and guests were jammed together, and the wait staff didn't have a lot of room to move through. Waiters had to sidestep while carrying trays of drinks or food.

The floor and walls vibrated from loud music. A DJ on the other side of the dance floor kept the mix going non-stop.

The Triple 8 kept the interior in low light, spotlights moving in circles around the dance floor, but the lights solid above the diners where Raven and Tracy sat. Glowing blue strips on the floor showed the path through the tables.

Raven sat so he could see the door. He tapped Tracy's hand after spotting Genest and Wagner. Genest was hard to miss with his belly and full head of dark hair. The taller Wagner stood out no matter how hard he tried not to. The German was also dressed in black, while Genest looked sharp in a tailored suit. Genest resembled a sixty-something banker trying to relive his glory days. He was the oldest person in the place, and Raven wondered if the fact made him uncomfortable. The pair headed straight for the flight of stairs to the upper deck. It was the VIP area; Genest had to have made a reservation, as nobody else occupied the space. Raven was glad they went up there. It made them easier to watch. Now all they had to do was wait and see if anybody showed up to try and talk to him. Somebody who looked like a young terrorist.

"We need to laugh," Tracy said. She leaned close so Raven understood her.

"Say something funny," he said.

"I mean it looks like we're breaking up or something. Everybody's going to be watching the Debbie Downers and it'll blow our cover."

"Throw a drink in my face. Yell you never want to see me again and storm out."

"Can you be serious?"

"I am being serious."

"We're both being way *too* serious," she said. "We're the only ones not acting like we're enjoying ourselves."

"It's loud, crowded, and these drinks are watered down. I'm sure as hell *not* enjoying myself, Tracy."

"Fake it. Be a method actor. Play a role."

"I'll start yelling for Stella, will that help?"

Tracy shook her head, but Raven cracked her stoic façade. She started laughing.

"There," he said. "Now we blend in."

18

CASSIANO LA BELLA NEEDED TO SEE GENEST FACE-TO-FACE. IF the old man wouldn't make a new deal over the telephone, Cassiano would show him an envelope full of cash to change his mind. Hopefully. He didn't want Genest and Wagner dead. There'd be no way to acquire another nuclear trigger set if they were dead, right? But there had to be a consequence if they told him no again. He'd show them the cash, ask them to make a deal, or perish. For Cassiano, it was more than a matter of pride. Everybody thought he was small fry. No. He'd show them, or die trying, how much he was worthy of the big time. He was worthy of being a major player. He was worthy of his name carrying a specter of fear whenever somebody spoke it out loud. That was the dream. You don't reach dreams by giving up and giving in when you hear the word no.

Cassiano had expected Simona to argue when he suggested they go to the club. She didn't. She walked into the club on his arm, dressed to kill, and the eyes landing on her were one of two types. Jealousy from the women, admiration from the men. Cassiano didn't mind. It made him invisible.

He was the wraith nobody noticed, until it was too late. He liked the idea a great deal. He had one of his gunners with him, a man named Sergio, from Spain. The bodyguard walked behind him, but Cassiano was aware of his presence. He had other gunners stationed down the street as a precaution. They were his last three shooters. The rest were dead. The rest hadn't survived this first mission, but Cassiano wouldn't let their deaths go in vain. He'd finish the mission in their memory, no matter what he had to do.

As they found a table in the crowded dining section, he glanced upward. At the upper deck. He saw only a partial view of two heads above the barrier, but he knew Genest was there.

He wanted to race up the steps. But he kept his mentor's advice in mind. *Take your time. But give no quarter when the time comes.* It was hard to think with such loud music assaulting his ears, but he worked at keeping his thoughts clear.

Cassiano scooted closer to Simona. He wanted to smell her perfume. Plus, he didn't want to have to yell to talk to her. She consulted the wine list. He wanted to dance, but she hated dancing. Sitting with her back to the dance floor she communicated she had no interest in stepping beyond the barrier.

He leaned closer to her. "What are you getting?"

"I'll start with a red," she told him.

Sergio, the bodyguard, shook his head when Cassiano raised an eyebrow at him. His job was to protect the boss, not indulge.

A waitress took their orders, and Cassiano turned to watch the bodies on the dance floor while Simona looked at her phone. He made sure not to let his eyes linger too long on any woman dancing, and there were plenty of attractive ladies to look at. She might have her eyes on the phone screen, but she'd see if he watched any of the other girls.

Movement on the upper deck caught his eye. There! Roch Genest, champagne in hand, stood looking at the dance floor like a king examining his subjects. *Very soon. Take your time.*

"GET A LOAD OF THIS TURKEY," Raven said.

While Tracy turned her head, Raven positioned his cell phone on the table to snap a picture of Cassiano La Bella.

"I don't recognize him," she said.

"He's somebody," Raven said. "The third wheel at the table isn't for show. He's a bodyguard."

"He hides his weapon well."

"Does he, though?"

"His sport coat is tailored, but I can tell what's underneath. If you didn't know he was packing a gun—"

"Yeah. But what do these three have in common with everyone else we've tangled with?"

"They're all the same age," Tracy said.

"Yup."

"Got the picture?"

"Got three pictures," Raven said. "Now I'll get one of the woman."

"Make sure you get her face and not only her tits. That dress could be a tube of toothpaste the way she's oozing out of it."

Raven laughed. He indeed snapped a picture of Simona's face, but he wasn't immune to the overall view of the low-cut party dress.

Raven held the phone under the table and examined the pictures. Satisfied with the result, he emailed them to Oscar

Morey with a request to ID both. He added they'd be connected to the dead guys in the morgue.

"How long do we have to wait?" Tracy asked.

"Can't do anything until they do something. Enjoy your drink."

"Don't mind if I do." She swallowed more of her gin and tonic.

"ONE DANCE?" Cassiano asked.

Simona glared at him. "No."

"Nobody is going to laugh at you."

"We aren't here to party, Cass," she told him.

"Well—"

"We can party when the mission is over."

"The mission will *never* be over."

"This one," she said.

"Sure." Cassiano looked up. Genest had retaken his seat and only the top of his head and the head of Wagner showed. They'd had a real shouting match over the telephone, but US greenbacks would stop even the most annoyed arms dealer from saying no.

Genest wasn't dumb enough to do any shooting in public, and neither was Cassiano. It was the one reason to attempt meeting. Professionals don't fight in the open unless they had to, unless there was no other choice. There'd be some shooting for sure if Genest refused, but not until Cassiano was ready.

"Let's go," he said. "It's time." He rose, buttoning his sport coat. He didn't want Genest to think he had a gun under his coat. He did, but the point was not to make it obvious. He didn't want the conversation to start on the wrong note.

This was the chance of a lifetime, and he didn't want to ruin it. He hoped Genest didn't ruin it for him.

Cassiano helped Simona to her feet and Sergio fell in step behind them. They followed the glowing tape on the floor to the opening in the rail and headed for the steps to the upper deck. Halfway up, Wagner appeared at the top and stopped them.

"Go away," the German said. His wire-framed glasses reflected one of the spotlights sweeping the dance floor.

"Mr. Wagner. Please ask Mr. Genest if he'll see me."

Cassiano hated looking up at the tall man, but there was no other choice.

"He won't."

Simona passed Cassiano the thick envelope she took from her purse. Cassiano opened it to show Wagner the US dollars inside. "Tell him I have cash. A lot of cash."

"What part of no don't you understand?"

Genest called out, "Wagner! Let him up."

Cassiano told Simona and Sergio to wait where they stood. He followed Wagner with a smile and a gleam in his eyes. This was his chance.

Roch Genest glared at him from his seat.

Cassiano's smile faded.

19

CASSIANO SAT IN THE CHAIR FORMERLY OCCUPIED BY WAGNER, who took up standing behind him. The younger man tried not to get nervous. He didn't want anybody standing out of eyesight. But he reminded himself they weren't going to shoot him or cut his throat in front of so many witnesses. How would they get rid of his body? And the bodies of Simona and Sergio? Genest wasn't so well connected as to get away with murder in public.

"You're a pest, do you know that?" Genest said. He raised his voice to be heard over the thump-bump of the club's soundtrack.

"I prefer the word persistent."

"I don't give two shits what you prefer, Mr. La Bella."

"All I want to do is give you money in exchange for a product. I'm not even asking for a refund of the money my men gave you earlier."

"You'd be a fool to try."

"What happened the other night wasn't the fault of you or your men. You held up your end of the bargain, no doubt. I'm here to give you more money for another set of triggers."

"What makes you think we have more?"

"I'm not blind. You sold us two triggers. There was only one in the original backpack nuke. You obviously reverse engineered a copy."

"Hmmm," Genest said.

"It isn't hard to do. If you made one, you made another. And another. No way would you waste such an opportunity to provide the one impossible piece of a nuclear bomb to acquire."

"You're not as dumb as I thought," Genest said.

"Can we do business a second time?"

"Absolutely not," Genest said. "You're not only reckless for coming to see me, but this entire situation has proven more trouble than it's worth. No. I don't care how much money you throw around. And, by the way? I know it's not your money. You're throwing around somebody else's cash. Tell me who your benefactor is and I might change my mind."

"I can't give you that information," Cassiano said.

"Then you have your answer. Now leave."

"But—"

"This conversation is over, and I'm not telling you again."

Genest stared at him without blinking, stared into Cassiano's eyes. Cassiano recognized the killer behind the stare. He gave up with a sigh. Now there was only one way to go, and he hated to do it, but he was a killer too. Killing Genest wouldn't solve his problem, but it would send a message. *Say no to Cassiano La Bella and die.*

The Frenchman had chosen his own fate. Cassiano was only there to seal the deal.

"Okay," Cassiano said. "I wish it didn't have to be this way."

Genest said nothing more. Cassiano stood and turned for the stairs. He met Simona and Sergio on the way down. The trio proceeded to the exit. The time for talk was over. Now it was time for vengeance.

———————

RAVEN SAID, "LET'S GET MOVING."

Tracy left her unfinished third drink on the table and followed Raven to the door. Nobody else but the man they were looking for would have gone to see Roch Genest.

And Genest had refused the attempt.

Raven had a feeling he knew what would happen next.

GENEST PAID his bill and tried to keep the disgust from showing on his face. Cassiano had ruined his evening. He was leaving way earlier than anticipated. The little brat thought he was something special, for sure. Genest wanted to show him he was nothing more than a bug who needed to be crushed. He jerked his head at Wagner and the two men left the club for the much less noisy outside. A long line still filled the sidewalk. Genest and Wagner waited for the Mercedes. The driver pulled up within two minutes. They climbed in and the driver accelerated into traffic.

Two men on motorcycles, watching the club, and having received Cassiano's signal, took off after Genest's car.

Raven and Tracy followed the motorcycles in their car.

Inside, Raven sat in the passenger seat while Tracy drove. He took the Nighthawk Custom .45 from the holster under his coat. "Stay with them."

"What's the plan? Or are we making it up as we go along?"

"We're winging this one," he said. "If those goons on the bikes start shooting, we take 'em out. I need Genest and Wagner walking free."

"You'll question them when the time is right?"

"You bet."

He was, if he wasn't careful, breaking Rule Two: No Gunfights in Public. But this was a case of ending a fight as soon as it started in order to keep civilians from getting hurt. If he shot fast enough, there'd be no innocent casualties. If he failed to stop the attack…

He had to.

There was no room for failure.

Tracy weaved through traffic to keep up with the motorcycles. Raven wondered when they'd start the fight. His reaction was based on their timing. And where was their boss? Probably long gone so as not to be associated with the death and destruction he'd ordered. Raven had a few choice words for the young man as well. He looked forward to meeting him face-to-face. Soon.

"Go faster," Genest said.

He spoke in response to the driver advising they had two motorcycles following them.

"Gotta give the kid some credit," Wagner said. He didn't bother to look behind them but took an H&K 9mm pistol from the holster on his right hip.

"We're going to deal with him permanently after this."

"Don't worry, I'll find him."

The driver yelled, "Incoming! Guns out!"

"Down!"

Genest and Wagner dropped low as the pair on the motorcycles roared up along either side of the car. They fired full-auto machine pistols. The bullets ripped into the body and shattered the back glass. Genest pulled the collar of his coat tight around his neck to keep shards from dropping down the back of his shirt. Wagner twisted around, extended his pistol out the back window, and fired once. He aimed at the motorcyclist on the driver's side. The rider was parallel with the back fender. Wagner's shot missed and whined off the wall of a building across the street.

Wagner frowned as a second car joined the fight. But the man who leaned out with a pistol of his own wasn't aiming at them. His gun muzzle focused on the motorcyclists.

Raven held his .45 steady despite the wind whipping at him. He braced his body in the open window frame. He didn't have the option of a miss. Cars behind them and to the side had braked hard in the first second of the shooting, but there was still traffic ahead. Raven fired twice. The first motorcyclist arched his back and his machine veered off the road to smash into a parked car. The rider tumbled over the roof of the car and landed with a smack on the sidewalk.

Tracy yelled for him to hang on. She followed the Mercedes as it swerved in and out of lanes. They blasted through a red light with other drivers screeching brakes and honking horns. Raven held tight as the road curved, Tracy keeping pace, the second motorcyclist swerving to stay with the Mercedes. The rider kept his weapon extended, but didn't waste ammo with indiscriminate firing.

The Mercedes slowed and cut left across the opposite lanes and jumped the curb into an alley. The motorcycle followed and so did Tracy. Raven ducked back inside as the alley walls flashed by. They'd have taken his head off. The car bumped and jolted as the tires crushed the debris on the alley floor; the motorcyclist weaved through the mess. Then the rider swung his machine pistol over his right shoulder and fired a burst. The shots bounced off the brick wall on the left side of the car and a few struck Tracy's side. *Smack smack.* They thudded into the bodywork. Tracy didn't flinch, and none of the shots hit glass. The rider tried again, and this time a few rounds bounced from the brick and skipped across the windshield, leaving jagged streaks behind. Tracy yelped. Raven threw up an arm to cover his face. But the danger passed as the Mercedes reached the end of the alley, swerving right, screeching tires and causing an immediate traffic jam as oncoming cars reacted. Metal crunched and glass shattered as several cars impacted with one another. The motorcycle blazed through unscathed while Tracy's wide turn almost brought them into a head-on crash with a truck in the opposite lane. She kept spinning the wheel, screeching back into the correct lane, and spun the wheel to straighten the car. The engine whined as she pressed the gas.

Raven slid out into the window frame again. The Nighthawk .45 remained hot in his hand.

Tracy caught up quick and Raven didn't waste time. He took aim. Another pair of shots. The second motorcyclist, still trying to fire through the gaping hole in the back of the Mercedes, didn't know what hit him. He pitched to the side, his motorcycle skidding across the pavement, kicking up a line of sparks. His body stopped when it slammed into a light post. The motorcycle ricocheted off the post and crashed through the window of a shop.

Raven made eye contact with Wagner. The German stared through the broken back window in disbelief. Raven put his gun away and waved, then ducked back into the car. Tracy took the next right and put the carnage behind them.

Inside Genest's Mercedes, Wagner sat forward. Genest sat upright again, brushing glass from his clothes.

"Well," the Frenchman said.

"We appear to have a mysterious helper," Wagner told him. He described Raven's attack.

"Great," the Frenchman muttered. "Another player on the chessboard. Is he on our side, or does he want something?"

"We'll find out."

"In the meantime," Genest said, "it's time to leave Tangier, don't you think?"

"What about La Bella?"

"He will pay for this outrage shortly."

20

CASSIANO LA BELLA PRESSED THE RED BUTTON ON HIS CELL screen, ending a call delivering the bad news. He set the phone on the kitchen counter with a shaking hand. Simona watched him with concern. She'd changed from the low-cut party dress to sweatpants and a sweatshirt. The outfit was too large for her and swallowed her curves.

"What happened?" she asked.

"There was somebody else. Somebody shot our men."

"Where did it come from? They only had the one car!"

"I don't understand either."

"What do we do now?"

"I don't know," he said.

"We have to call Graham."

"It's all falling apart, Simona. And the council—I don't know what's going to happen when they find out. I'm surprised they haven't already, with all the men we lost."

"Look, it's late, we can't decide anything right now. Let's get to bed and figure this out in the morning. Don't call Graham until tomorrow morning."

"Do you think I can sleep after this?"

"Do you think I can?" She shrugged. "At least we'll be together. Come on."

With no other choice except to pace and mope all night, he followed her. With the loft silent, Simona on her side in bed, Cassiano lay on his back and stared at the ceiling. How was he missing so many details? Variables he couldn't plan for, like the second car, kept interfering with otherwise text-book plans. Wait…the second car hadn't been part of Roch Genest's crew. The American, Sam Raven, stuck his nose and his gun into their business once again. Had to be him.

He'd indeed contact Graham first thing in the morning. If they were going to succeed, Sam Raven first needed to die.

WHEN CASSIANO DELIVERED the news to Evan Graham over the phone, the CIA man's first reaction was to call the younger man incompetent. But he didn't, because Cassiano ended his story with the theory of Raven being the one in the second car.

Which meant Tracy was there, too.

"We need to get rid of Raven," Cassiano stressed. "First. Now. Nothing will work if he's around."

"Our sponsor is sending help," Graham said. He knew what was coming next…

"No! We will handle this."

"How many gunners do you have left, Cassiano? You didn't bring an army."

Cassiano paused a moment, and Graham didn't prompt him. Instead, he went to the hotel room's coffee maker and began preparing one of the pre-packaged brews. He placed a paper cup under the spout and pressed the START button.

"You still there?" Graham said.

"It's only me and Simona and one other man. All I have

left. You have to let us do this and let us take back what he took from us."

"What did he take from you, Cassiano?"

"Are you joking? He's killed my friends. He's ruining my chance to score a victory against capitalism. Do I really have to explain this? Everything is on the line! Sam Raven is destroying what I've worked so hard to achieve."

Graham grinned. He appreciated Cassiano mentioning his dead friends first, but the rest...

He was young with a big ego and big ideas and learning the hard way the world didn't give a damn about his revolution. And his "terrorist celebrity" scheme was so off base, Graham didn't know where to begin his criticism. Graham figured he'd be reduced to taking selfies with his girlfriend next to a car bomb. *'Bout to blow up this car for realz so smash that like and follow for more*, or some shit.

"When our sponsor's man arrives," Graham said, "we can talk about it further."

The coffee maker began dripping coffee into the plastic cup. A steady drizzle. Graham watched with full attention.

"All right," Cassiano said. "But I'm serious. He needs to go!"

"I agree. Give me a few more hours."

Somebody knocked at the hotel room door. Three light taps.

"In fact," Graham continued, "I think he's here now."

"Call me back."

"I will."

Graham ended the call and dropped the phone on the bed. The coffee maker stopped dribbling and beeped; his coffee was ready. The aroma filled the room. Graham pulled the door open and blinked at the man standing in the hallway.

The new arrival was short, with a jowly face, poor-looking skin. His hair was shaggy without being long like Graham's. His clothes were baggy and nothing anybody would remember. Plain jeans, faded. T-shirt hidden under an ugly green jacket. Graham expected him to be Canadian and speak with an accent. He didn't and wasn't.

"Evan Graham?"

"Yeah."

"I'm supposed to say the snow is melting...then you finish."

"In Arizona."

"Yeah, that's the code. Silly, huh?" He chuckled. "It doesn't snow in Arizona." A frown. "Right?"

"Come in."

Graham stepped back to allow the short man to enter. He asked, "What do I call you?"

"I'm Jack. Jack Moss. Don't worry, I don't always look this sloppy. It's all part of my clever disguise."

Graham started to smile. He decided he'd been wrong to distrust Harrison Hunt's suggestion of help. "I just made coffee; do you want it?"

"I can only do decaf. I get the jitters really bad otherwise."

"I think I have decaf…"

Graham turned to the coffee maker and examined the other packages. Moss's right arm moved a certain way, toward his left armpit; it only meant one thing. Graham had been wrong to think Jack Moss was harmless; he wasn't. His first instinct was the correct one. Harrison Hunt wanted him dead. Well, Evan Graham had the opposite point of view, and he went into action to make his case.

Moss had his compact pistol, fitted with a suppressor, half out of the armpit holster. Graham grabbed for Moss's gun arm, pinning it between them, forcing the muzzle under Moss's chin. Moss reacted, twisting his body to break Graham's grip, which sent his gun arm swinging toward the bed. Moss brought a knee into Graham's groin. The CIA man bit off a cry, but he kept going. With his left hand keeping Moss's gun arm away, he used his left to smack the jowly man in the face. Moss recoiled back, pulling Graham with him. Graham kicked Moss's feet out from under him. The killer crashed against the dresser and fell onto the floor near the foot of the bed. Graham straddled the killer, grabbing for the suppressed pistol, about to wrench it from Moss's hand when Moss punched him. Stunned, Graham didn't move for a second. Moss jammed his gun into Graham's midsection and fired, then fired again and again. Graham didn't hear the shots that killed him, but death registered on his face immediately.

THE DEAD CIA man plopped against the bed. Jack Moss scooted back from the body. He remained on the carpet for a moment, catching his breath, thinking next time he should be a little further away when he shot somebody so as not to end up in a hand-to-hand fight. Standing, he stepped over Graham and went to the coffee maker, picking up the cup Graham had prepared.

"I don't get the jitters," he said to the dead man. He sipped the coffee and nodded. Not bad for pre-packaged. He put away his pistol and held on to the coffee as he departed. The hotel room door clicked shut behind him. As he walked down the hall, he used his free hand to extract a cell phone from his left jacket pocket, pressed a button, and held the phone to his ear. The pickup came after three rings.

"Hey, it's Jack. Tell Mr. H the job is done, and I'm moving onto the next one."

He didn't wait for a reply. Moss put the phone away and

took the stairs back to the lobby. He was careful not to spill his coffee on the way down.

CASSIANO LA BELLA sat at the dining table off the kitchen, lost in a cycle of negative thoughts surrounding his situation and contemplated leaving. Hell with the revolution. Let somebody else fight the war. It wasn't worth the cost, which Montego had tried to tell him. But he hadn't been listening.

No. Quitting isn't the way. Getting this far has cost us too much to quit.

The phone rang.

Cassiano frowned at the unknown number from the United States. He almost didn't answer and let to call go to voicemail. Instinct suggested otherwise.

"Yes?"

"Is this Mr. La Bella?"

The voice was deep, the accent American for sure. A contact of Graham's?

"Yes."

"Mr. La Bella, you don't know who I am. But I know you. To date, you've been dealing with my associate Evan Graham. I regret to inform you my partnership with Mr. Graham has ended."

Cassiano left the table and moved away from the windows. It was stupid to have sat there anyway. He moved around a corner, out of view from the glass. "In what way is he no longer associated with you?"

"You know what way. It's why you got away from the glass, Mr. La Bella."

"You're watching me?"

"Yes indeed. Another partner of mine has a video camera

on your loft. I'm watching you from across the ocean and sending my other associate to see you."

"To kill me?"

"Not at all," the man on the phone said. "He's taking Graham's place. We still have work to do, my friend. I need you. Let's not get bogged down talking about the late unpleasantness; it's not productive. What we need to do is keep our eyes on the future."

"We have to kill Sam Raven."

"Mr. Raven is a mere annoyance and will also serve a purpose. We only have to keep him at bay."

"I don't understand."

"You will shortly. Let my associate into the loft. His name is Jack Moss. He'll explain everything and act as your guide through the next steps."

"I don't think I will."

"Mr. La Bella—"

"How am I supposed to trust you when you won't trust me?"

"What do you want?"

"You name."

"I see."

"Graham only referred to you as our sponsor," Cassiano said.

"You'll recognize my name, Mr. La Bella. I am Harrison Hunt."

Cassiano laughed.

"Please share the joke," the American said.

"I thought your voice sounded familiar."

The kitchen intercom buzzed. Somebody was on the sidewalk trying to gain access to the building.

"Please allow Jack into the loft," Hunt said. "He will tell you everything you need to know."

"If he kills me, expect visitors, Mr. Hunt."

"Why would I talk to you if I wanted you dead? Jack could have shot you through the window. You were sitting there for two hours."

"All right. I'll let him in." Cassiano crossed to the kitchen and pressed a button on the intercom panel. The button activated a switch at street level to unlock the doors. He called for Simona to join him. When he spoke into the phone again for a final word with Harrison Hunt, he stopped short. Hunt had already disconnected.

OSCAR MOREY CALLED Raven and said he had urgent news.

"What is it?" Raven asked.

"The picture you sent. I got a name. Cassiano La Bella. He's connected to the guys you shot at the Airbnb and he's also a student of Ernesto Montego and held an internship at the Council of Economic Equality."

"How is he connected with the others?"

"Classmates. Free University of Berlin."

"All right," Raven said. "It sounds like Berlin is our next stop."

"You're not going to spend any more time with Genest?"

"Already gone. They took off for points unknown this morning."

"What are you going to tell the CIA?"

"I'll fill them in once we get to Berlin. They have a mess to clean up in Tangier and by the time they're done, this will be over."

"You hope."

Raven said, "I sure do."

"Don't you want to take a run at La Bella before you go?"

"What do you mean?"

"I found where he's staying. He and a woman named

Simona Vadala rented a loft not too far from you. They used their real names."

"You didn't think to lead with this information, Oscar?"

"You want the address or not?"

"Yes. I'll pay a visit and we won't be bringing a bottle of wine."

TRACY THOUGHT the lead was too easy.

"How does Oscar know for sure?"

"La Bella rented the place in his own name," Raven told her as he drove. It was early evening. Traffic was heavy, but the delays brief.

"Really? Rookie move."

"True, but nobody's looking for him. His name doesn't have any dirt on it. In a way, it makes sense."

"But he didn't think about the future. He wasn't planning—"

"On us."

Raven slowed the car as he neared La Bella's address and passed the building where he and Simona were staying. He made a right turn and looked for parking, but every space on either side of the street was taken. Raven circled the block twice before he gave up and found a parking spot curbside two blocks away. Blending with the evening foot traffic on the sidewalk, they walked back to La Bella's building. They stopped on the corner across the street. Raven looked up at the loft windows at the top of the building.

"What is it?" Tracy asked. "Other than it looks dark up there."

"I suppose they could be out on the town."

"Not after last night."

"You think they took off?" he asked.

"After trying to whack Genest? Wouldn't you?"

"Yeah," Raven said absently. He turned.

The building entrance behind them belonged to another apartment complex. Raven and Tracy went inside. Quiet lobby. A bank of elevators around a corner. They rode up to the top floor. Raven told Tracy he wanted to find access to the roof, get a better look at the loft. Exiting on the top floor, they found a stairwell but had to negotiate over a locked baby gate to get to the flight of steps leading to the roof access door. The door's dead bolt blocked them next. Raven used a set of lock picks to twist the lock open, and they stepped onto the roof. Light wind blew against them, but it was warm.

"Nice view," Tracy said.

It was tempting to stop and look out at the city lights, ocean sounds in the distance, but Raven had other priorities in mind. They went to the side of the roof facing La Bella's building, and the darkness of the upper loft only confirmed what Raven deduced from the street. They were too late; the lot was empty; Cassiano La Bella and whoever remained of his crew had departed. Probably in a hurry.

Tracy said, "All we need is a couple of grappling hooks to shoot over and we can slide across. Slip in, check the place out, shoot some bad guys. Sound like fun?"

"That's funny," Raven said, distracted, focused on the loft.

"What are you thinking?"

"Enjoy your last view of Tangier. We need to get to Berlin and talk to La Bella's professor, this Montego fellow. Because, otherwise, the trail just ended, and I'll be damned if I'm going to let them get away."

21

NEITHER RAVEN NOR TRACY SPOKE ON THE FLIGHT TO BERLIN.

They woke up in the morning to news of Graham's murder, leaving Tracy in a shocked state of silence. Raven was willing to let her stay there as long as she required. They flew on his private jet, a Cessna Citation CJ3. The pilots were a pair of mercenaries Raven kept on the payroll. They'd flown him back and forth across the world several times over the years. They knew how to keep their mouths shut between jobs, too. Raven's money came from two sources. Sometimes, people hired him; he charged a high amount for his services. When the CIA or MI6 was paying the bills, he charged the company an equally high amount. Other times, when working on his own, he found ways to steal the enemy's money. They always seemed to have large amounts of cash laying around for grabbing hands like his. Especially when they were no longer alive to use the money themselves.

Raven sat in a plush leather chair near a window, watching the ground far below. He had other choices for entertainment on board but preferred the quiet. The hum of the twin jet engines within the cabin was the only noise. It was a soothing sound.

Finally, Tracy dropped into the seat across from him.

"Are you okay?" he asked her.

"I wanted to shoot Graham myself."

"At least we know the truth."

"But who ordered him killed? I don't think for one minute Cassiano La Bella is in charge. He doesn't look old enough to shave."

"We'll find the puppet master."

"If the CIA doesn't hamstring us."

"Not my problem," Raven said. "The Agency doesn't give me orders."

"They're wondering where I am right now."

"I'll have to tell Clark what's going on," he said. "You should go by the book, too. Check in with the embassy when we get to Berlin. Refer them to Clark if they have questions."

"They will," Tracy said. "The Berlin station chief doesn't like surprises. Especially when there's blowback from an operation in progress."

"Don't worry about the Agency. Our best bet is to hit the Council for Economic Equality. I have a feeling the entire outfit is an extremist front."

"They must hide it well."

"With a veteran like Ernesto Montego at the helm, we shouldn't be surprised."

"Is he the big boss, though? Can he organize the cash La Bella needed to buy those triggers?"

"We'll find out," Raven said.

"I owe my team, Raven. Promise you won't quit on me."

"You'll pay your debt. But keep one thing in mind."

"What?"

"You can pay the debt a million times, but you'll never feel like you've settled the account."

"Is that a fact?"

"Don't doubt me. It's an unfortunate fact. You have to learn to live with it."

"I live with a lot already."

"We all do," he said. "And every time something happens, like the ambush you experienced, we add a little more."

Tracy's face softened. She said, "Does it get better?"

"You've been searching for your father a long time. Has it become easier for you?"

"No."

"There's your answer."

The pilot's voice over the intercom broke into the conversation. They were thirty minutes from Berlin. Tracy left the chair and returned to her previous seat. Raven turned his head to look out the window.

The answer never changed, as much as he wished it would. There was no use complaining. The only thing he knew how to do was get on with the job. And as he saw it, the job was simple.

Find Cassiano La Bella.

Find the puppet master.

Stop them.

THEY CLEARED customs under their own names. Raven didn't see any reason to use an alias; they weren't on any wanted lists. With Tracy checking in with the CIA station at the US Embassy, there was even less reason to hide their entry. Raven told his pilots to stand by as usual. How they spent their time wasn't his concern; but as always, he needed them ready to leave without a lot of notice. So far, the pair had never argued with him.

Raven and Tracy, luggage in hand, finally made it to the

end of the taxi line. Raven gave the driver the name of the hotel he'd booked prior to leaving Tangier. The Berlin Brandenburg Airport was south of the city sharing its name in Schonefeld. It wasn't a long trip into central Berlin, but traffic stretched the travel time to longer than Raven wanted. Tracy remained quiet during the drive. When the taxi finally pulled up at the Berlin Marriott, Raven suggested they check in and eat. They were both ready for a break. Raven hoped Tracy didn't stay detached and consumed with her thoughts for much longer. There was a lot of work to do and it was going to get rough very fast.

As they ate in the hotel restaurant, Tracy said, "We need a cover."

"What do you suggest?"

"An easy one. We go see Montego and tell him we're journalists. Reporters for a such-and-such commie rag that wants to highlight what he and the council are doing."

"I don't know of any commie rags off the top of my head."

"I'll talk to Wilson. He can have an online thing made up quickly. Fill it with all kinds of socialist crap. Montego will eat it up. All we need to do is get close to him and—"

"Stick a gun in his belly? Why not skip the charade?"

"Am I overthinking this?"

"You wanted an easy cover. How about no cover at all? The longer we take, the further ahead La Bella gets. Let's do some surveillance on Montego, see where he goes and who he meets, and then pounce."

"No winging it this time?"

"No," Raven said.

22

SIMONA WASN'T SURE SHE TRUSTED JACK MOSS AND SAID SO, quietly, to Cassiano in the middle of the flight. He tried to shush her with a dismissive wave; it didn't work.

"Don't tell me to shut up."

"What else can we do?" Cassiano glanced around the cabin to make sure Moss wasn't close. "You want to finish this mission or not?"

"I don't want this Harrison Hunt, if that's who you really spoke with, to find a place to dump our bodies when he's done with us."

Cassiano started to answer, then laughed instead. Simona frowned and then saw the reason. His laugh covered the heavy footsteps of Jack Moss as he returned from the cockpit. Cassiano met Moss's glance as he saw a smile on the other man's face.

They were on their way to Oslo, Norway, in a private jet. The walkway wasn't as wide as a commercial airliner. Cassiano wondered how comfortable the cabin would be full of passengers. With only him and Simona, Moss and Sergio, Cassiano's last remaining shooter, there wasn't any overcrowding. Sergio sat in the back of the plane, by himself, with instructions to keep an eye on Moss and his movements. Cassiano understood Simona's distrust, but there was no other way to accomplish the mission.

They'd departed Tangier in a hurry. Moss gave them enough time to pack, but they'd left a few things behind at the loft. Nothing important, but the items included food and other supplies and Cassiano hated the idea of food going to waste. The landlord would toss everything once it spoiled, if not before. For him, the old adage of "people starving in China" rang true. He wanted a world where nothing vital went to waste, everybody had a fair share, where everybody thrived because nobody starved. It was a goal spoken often, but as yet never achieved, because those who did the talking didn't have the wherewithal to do anything but talk. It was easier to claim you were fighting for the underdog while raking in cash to live like a king. Cassiano wanted the exact opposite. When he was in charge…

When indeed.

Moss sat in the seat facing Cassiano and Simona. He still wore frumpy clothes. He wanted to pass himself off as the Great Nobody. Cassiano had to admit he did the job well.

Moss said, "We should be landing in a little over an hour."

"Good," Cassiano said. "Then what?"

"We'll meet again with Mr. Genest and Mr. Wagner. It won't be in a way they'll appreciate, though. It'll be like setting off a stink bomb during a bar mitzvah." Moss laughed.

"Fine with me. I'm done talking. There's been too much talking already."

Simona said, "What about the Americans? Raven and the woman."

"What about them?" Moss said. "They're nowhere near here. They're a bouncing ball looking for a place to land, and they may land on Mom's antique vase. Break it into a thousand pieces. There's never enough glue to fix those things, you know. In fact, the only option they have will take them far away from us."

Cassiano felt a sense of dread. "Wait—"

"It has to happen sometime, Cassiano."

"But them going to Professor Montego? It that necessary?"

"What does he know?" Moss asked. "The professor. What can he tell them?"

"Nothing."

"Are you sure?"

"He knows nothing, I swear. I've been worried about him discovering us since we started."

"Why?"

"It's—it's not what he'd want."

"You look scared, Cassiano."

The younger man wanted to smack Moss hard enough to scramble his brain. He took a breath to regain his composure.

"You don't know what it's like," he said.

"What's like?"

"Letting somebody down."

"Oh, he trusted you, did he? Expect more from you? Told you not to become a wild gunman fighting the same crusade he served time in prison for?"

Cassiano tried to answer but the words jammed in his throat.

The jowly Moss cracked a grin. "I know all too well what it's like to disappoint somebody. One person in particular told me to my face. Before he died."

"Before you killed him?"

"Yes," Moss said.

Cassiano felt Simona's left hand touch his right. He grasped hers softly.

"Becoming what you want," Moss continued, "requires sacrifices. Bridges need to burn. How much does your cause mean to you?"

"I'm curious about your cause. What are you dedicated to?"

"Never mind me," Moss said. "I asked you the question."

Cassiano tightened his grip on Simona's hand.

"We're all in. Whatever it takes."

"Then it's going to take letting down Professor Montego. But the glory you'll find will soothe any bad feelings. You'll see."

"You going to answer my question?" Cassiano asked.

"Later," Moss said. "For now, we need to talk about Genset and Wagner. Gotta make plans. Talk strategy, you know. Efficient use of our time and all that."

"First priority," Cassiano said, "is to get another set of nuclear triggers."

He wasn't going to let Moss forget his question. Moss was fighting for somebody or something, for sure. But Cassiano wondered if that something or somebody was himself and nobody else.

"And then we kill them both," Moss said.

Cassiano grinned.

"I like the way you think," the younger man said.

Simona let go of his hand.

23

HER NAME WAS LIA KENISOVA, AND SHE DIDN'T GO AFTER small fish.

She was a Russian covert specialist, freelancer, as deadly as she was stunning, and had come to the aid of her country for a specific mission. She needed to track down a missing backpack nuke. And a major lead waited for her in a Moscow nightclub.

When Lia left home to join the Russian army and later GRU, the military intelligence apparatus, she'd avoided her family's financial failings—her father's in particular—filling her pockets via the graft and corruption running rampant in the Russian government.

Using her nest egg to launch a freelance career, she was now in high demand as a retrieval specialist, gun girl, Jill-of-all-covert-trades. Her resume included counter-terrorist activity to protect her country from those who wanted to destroy it. She relished every kill preventing casualties to the Motherland.

She'd been hired for her current job because the Kremlin needed deniability. They didn't want an official investigation into the stolen backpack nuke, which meant the best way to go about such a task was to hire an outsider.

Lia had spent the last couple of weeks going through every lead she could find within her own country, with the goal of learning how the nuke left Russian borders and, most important, who facilitated its movement.

She entered Night Flight, one of the best clubs in Moscow, where the elite wined and dined. It was the place you wanted to be if you could get past the bruiser of a bouncer at the front door. All Lia had to do was smile and the big man lifted the barrier to entry. A chorus of hoots from those still in line assaulted her ears, but Lia knew what they didn't. The bouncer was an SVR operative planted at the club. His job, getting her inside, was done. Now he'd stand there and screw with everybody in line.

Lia was dressed to kill. Slinky red dress, red lipstick, heels. The strapless top pressed her breasts together to create the perfect valley for a schmuck to get lost in should his eyes drift there. The diamond pendant around her neck promised a few glances too. Her long auburn hair, curled to perfection, drifted down her back and tickled her slender neck.

Loud music thump-bumped as she moved through the crowd. The hot temperature inside was a welcome change after the chill of the Moscow night. She hadn't brought a coat or a wrap.

Lots of bodies; some dancing. Others at tables crowded together, pressed elbow-to-elbow without any hint of privacy. You didn't come to *Night Flight* to have dinner by candlelight. The low light and strobe flashes from the dance floor had a way of taking you out of reality, but Lia wasn't about to let down her guard.

Her target sat at the bar and looked to be on his sixth vodka tonic.

Peter Kryukov was only a little taller than Lia. Blond hair, a square jaw, decent physique for somebody who worked in an office all day. There was another couple next to him, on his right. Two women. She was about to elbow the bitches out of the way when they left the bar to join friends at a table.

Lia took the stool beside Kryukov and ordered a martini.

The music wasn't as loud in the bar, but she still felt the floor vibrating through the legs of the barstool.

The bartender brought her martini, and she took the glass by the bowl, sipping the icy elixir. She examined her long, sharp fingernails. The red motif continued on the polish. She was Russian, after all.

"You look like an apple."

Lia turned her head slowly to raise an eyebrow at Kryukov's awkward opening line. He slurred most of the words.

"If I eat you every day, will it keep the doctor away?"

He laughed.

Lia couldn't help but smile. He'd done half of her job for her, and she had him on the hook.

"Those are the worse lines I have ever heard," she said.

"Do you hear a lot of them?"

"Men usually don't talk until I let them."

"Oh, so you like being in control. Will you tie me up before I eat you?"

She gave him a sour look. "Get some dinner if you're hungry." She started to scoot off the stool, but he grabbed her arm.

"Please. Forgive me. I'm sorry. It's been a long day. I didn't mean to offend."

Lia shook her head. Men apologized too much. Their appeal dropped a little in her book each time it happened. Once in her life, she wanted to meet a man who messed up in some way and said "tough shit" instead of "I'm sorry."

She held his gaze a moment and almost detected a pleading look in his eye. Good grief, he was a fish all right, much easier to hook than expected.

"All right, you get another chance."

He smiled, showing his teeth. It was a nice smile. Shame what might happen to it before the night ended.

Unless he cooperated.

She finished her martini, and he ordered her another and told the bartender to put the first one on his tab, too. Then they started a normal conversation. Kryukov told her all about his job with oil magnate Dusa Gusin. Lia pretended not to know the name. The oil magnate was the reason she had Kryukov, Gusin's number two man, on her target list this evening.

Gusin was the son of one of the Russian team tasked with recovering backpack nukes from the US at the end of the Cold War, but who instead stole the weapon and doctored inventory records to erase its official existence. He'd helped his father sell the weapon to the arms dealers who now sought to profit off the individual parts all these years later. Kryukov was his public representative in the deal; Gusin himself stayed in the background.

Kryukov didn't ask about her work. He figured her for a prostitute. The less he asked, the less she had to invent. She had a cover story ready, but he was already playing in to her hand, and all she had to do was reel him in.

Which she did, after a third martini and whatever umpteenth vodka tonic he swallowed. He handled his liquor well. Talking to her seemed to sharpen him. He only slurred a few words, and he managed to walk straight after she suggested they leave the noisy club.

And go somewhere private.

He had a company car and called the driver on his cell. They waited at the curb for about ten minutes, the line outside growing longer, the bouncer refusing to let anybody in. Lia didn't make any eye contact with the bouncer. If she ever saw him again on the job, she wouldn't remember his face anyway.

She told Kryukov to give the driver her apartment address. He didn't do as much talking as she figured he would. He'd gone from chatterbox to quiet.

To get his attention again, she put her hand on his leg and slowly moved it across the fabric of his slacks to his crotch. She squeezed.

He grunted, shifting. But he didn't respond.

She withdrew her hand and decided to wait until he figured out whatever he was planning to do.

Her plan was already well in motion.

All she needed was him, in her apartment, with a drink in his hand.

The driver made a final turn, went one more block, and pulled over in front of her building. With a smile, she beckoned him to follow her out of the car.

He didn't need any further encouragement.

The glass walls of Lia's apartment overlooked the bright lights of the city.

Kryukov put his hands on his hips and admired the view while she mixed drinks. He started idle chit-chat about how long she'd lived there. She gave short answers while making sure his attention was on the city lights. She palmed a vial from the back of her neck where she'd taped it. Her curly hair had concealed the vial. Cracking the cap open, Lia poured the clear contents into the vodka tonic.

She moved to the couch, positioned to face the glass wall and the view, and clicked her tongue to get his attention. He smiled and crossed to her, taking his drink. They clinked glasses. She sipped her glass while he took a long drink of his.

Perfect.

"Sit down."

He placed the glass on the table in front of the couch and sat down to watch her.

She stood in front of him and coyly bit her lower lip and he regarded her with eager eyes.

"Want to reach up my dress?"

"Sure."

"Move your right hand."

Kryukov blinked as he made the effort. His hand did not move.

"Um."

"Move your left leg."

"I can't."

Panic.

Lia sat on the table, crossing her legs.

"I've poisoned you," she said. "I will only give you the antidote if you answer my questions."

"What?"

"As you can see, you can still talk, but the rest of your body is paralyzed."

He strained to move any part of his body. He started to sweat.

"You work with a man named Gusin."

"Yes."

"Gusin used you to make a deal with arms dealers. For a portable nuclear weapon that belongs to the Motherland, not you or him."

Kryukov tried to nod, couldn't. He said, "Yes." More panic now. Sweat dripped down the side of his face.

"The poison will take twenty-four hours to kill you."

Kryukov let out a high-pitched squeal. Lia laughed.

"Tell me who you sold the weapon to."

Kryukov rushed out the answer. "A Frenchman! His name is Genest! He has a place in Oslo!"

"Where in Oslo?"

"I don't know! I swear!"

"You better tell me," she said.

Kryukov blurted out an address. His first attempt was garbled, his words rushed together. She made him slow down and repeat the information. There was no need to write it down. Lia committed the address to memory.

"Thank you, Peter."

"*Help me!*"

Kryukov made another squeal, sweating profusely now. Lia didn't blink as she watched him. She found the man's state fascinating. He was convinced she was going to let him die.

"If I give you the antidote, what are you going to do?" she asked.

"Go home!"

"And?"

"Never tell anybody about this!"

"Good boy."

Lia reached between her breasts where she'd taped the second vial. She broke the cap and leaned over Kryukov, forcing his mouth open. She poured the liquid onto his tongue and pushed his mouth closed. Kryukov swallowed.

Lia sat on the table again. "There. Was that so hard?"

Kryukov stared at her and waited for movement to return to his limbs. When it did, he lunged, but she'd expected such a move. An elbow strike to the temple toppled Kryukov to the carpet.

24

FEEDING PIGEONS IN MOSCOW WASN'T FROWNED UPON, BUT nobody encouraged it, either, and nobody tried to stop you if you insisted. Do-gooders in Russia wanted to protect wild animals from foods they shouldn't eat, so the rule was, if you're going to feed pigeons, make sure it was something similar to what they'd eat in the wild anyway. Ruslan Malikov thought the fuss was silly and paid no attention—he was old enough that nobody wanted to bother the pudgy old man who sat alone on a bench with a bag of breadcrumbs. He'd been feeding pigeons in Moscow for decades. First, with his grandfather, who took to the task when faced with a problem. Feeding pigeons, he said, always helped him solve the problem. The pigeons didn't interrupt when he tried to talk out what was on his mind, unlike people. When Malikov joined the ranks of Russian intelligence, the KGB, and later the FSB, he kept his grandfather's words in mind. Feeding pigeons always unlocked elusive solutions to complex problems. It was like magic. But Malikov kept the magic to himself.

He'd become wrapped up in the problem of what to do

with those responsible for stealing a backpack nuke several decades ago—when Ruslan Malikov was a younger man, when the men involved were younger men. Many years had passed and now they were old men and with one dying, what to do with the other two? He'd become so trapped in the problem-solving process he realized he'd forgotten to bring a bag of bread for the pigeons as he took his seat on a park bench somewhere in downtown Moscow. It was a sunny day, but chilly. He wore a heavy coat.

"I'm sorry, my friends," he said, as pigeons waddled in his direction. They gathered around him like a puddle. He wasn't sure if they recognized him or assumed anybody at the bench was going to feed them. He sighed heavily. He felt stupid. He should have remembered or asked his wife to remind him—too much work, too much on his mind. Missing nuclear weapons. My goodness, couldn't the world get over The Bomb? There always seemed to be somebody making a mad dash to build one or acquire one and for what? They held no value. All they did was destroy.

His black fur hat kept his bare skull warm, and he looked left and right for his contact. He was meeting Lia Kenisova to talk about her mission. The person or team investigating had to be Russians and had to understand the need for discretion. Top priority was making sure Russia wasn't blamed for an incident, which made the bomb's recovery the second priority.

It makes sense to somebody, Malikov decided upon his selection to lead the investigation. Logic and Russian politics were often mutually exclusive.

He oversaw the effort, but too old to go chasing villains. Enter Lia Kenisova. She was one of the bright lights of Russian intelligence in the last few years. A standout student during training, highly effective on assignment. She'd somehow figured out how to get rich as a freelancer; she had a lot to teach them all.

The park had its share of trees and grass. Malikov sat under a canopy of said trees and watched young men playing football on the grass. Elsewhere stood observant mothers watching their children on the swing set and slides. He might as well have been a grandfather on an afternoon stroll. He grinned at the implied cover. Nobody would look at him twice. Not even the pigeons gathered at his feet, who were still waiting for snacks.

"I forgot," he told them. Didn't matter. They waddled and cooed and did pigeon things.

"Looks like you need a rescue, Ruslan."

The older man looked right. He smiled. Lia Kenisova approached, clutching a brown paper bag along with her purse. She handed him the bag.

"I thought you might forget."

"You're wonderful, my dear," he said. The pigeon activity increased as Malikov opened the bag. He began tossing diced pieces of white bread at the puddle of pigeons. The flying rats began pecking at the morsels and made them disappear.

"These are fresh," he told her, tossing another handful.

"Fresh yesterday. I cut them myself."

"You're too good to me. My day would not have been complete if I let my little friends down."

She sat beside him and crossed her legs. She wore dark clothes. Black top, gray sweater, black stockings, and boots. Dark sunglasses. Walking monochrome. But she'd be noticed, no matter what. Lia Kenisova could walk around in a potato sack and she'd stand out.

"How did it go last night?" Malikov asked.

"Kryukov answered my questions."

Malikov tossed more bread. Pigeons cooed and rushed the new handful. "I won't ask how."

"I didn't hurt him," she said. "Much."

"Where are you going next?"

"Oslo. But I'm going to need help."

"I can find you help."

"No, Ruslan. I want to recruit my own people."

"Russians?"

"No, but I trust them like brothers." Lia shifted on the hard bench. But she communicated no discomfort.

"We'd prefer we kept this matter—"

"You told me when you hired me."

"All right," Malikov said. "Hire who you want. Anything else?"

"These pigeons are gross."

He let out a low chuckle and tossed more bread. Raising his voice, he told the pigeons not to listen to the mean lady. Then he turned to Lia and smiled.

"Good luck, my dear," he said. "Keep me posted through the usual means."

Lia nodded. She stood and made a kicking gesture at several pigeons who approached. Malikov tossed bread near her feet and more pigeons swarmed. She quick-stepped out of their path and gave the older man a look over her shoulder that was part reprimand and part admiration for a joke she should have expected.

LIA FACED FORWARD as she walked across the grass, up the gentle slope, to the street. She'd parked her car at the curb. With the conversation done, she was free to think of her next moves. Get help. Two of the best, indeed.

First call: an Armenian mercenary named Zaven Darbinian, "Darbo" to his friends.

Second call: Roger Justice, an American freelance black ops veteran with an appropriate surname.

Lia knew them through their work with Sam Raven. Raven christened them his "Raiders" and called on them when he faced a tough situation and needed more firepower. She wondered if she should give Sam a ring as well. Lia decided to let him lounge at home, if he were so doing; she doubted it. Raven wasn't the lounge around type. He was probably up to his eyeballs in a different situation than hers. She'd call if she needed another gunner and hope for the best. He was probably too busy. For now, Darbo and Roger were all she required.

Dropping behind the wheel of her car, she took a moment to dial and talk to each one.

ZAVEN DARBINIAN THOUGHT the basement ceiling looked rough and unfinished. The thick pipes seemed well sealed, however. It would have been awful to have a leak. He didn't get a chance to tell his host any of his observations, though.

A man on either side of him grabbed Darbo and hauled him off the floor and out of his knocked-over chair. He'd managed to lean forward as the chair fell so as not to bang his head on the concrete floor, which matched the ceiling, he noticed. The fall instead made his back hurt, but he was used to his back being sore a lot. The two goons stood him upright, and his eyes landed on the face of a third man. Darbo had to look down a little, because he was taller than the three men closest to him, as well as the two others still seated at the poker table.

The short man in front of Darbo was the owner of the house, Sasoun Garcha. He wore a blue tracksuit with white stripes down the sides of the pants. There were brown spots on the top of his bald head Darbo wanted to tell him to get examined, just in case. But Garcha didn't want to hear any of Darbo's advice. He stuck a gun in Darbo's belly, and when he spoke, his tone wasn't friendly.

"Why are you here?"

Darbo struggled against the tough grips of the other two men, who held his arms. They held him well. But they didn't have his legs.

"I'm only here for poker, my friend. I don't know why you suddenly got the ick about me."

"The ick? Twelve-year-old girls talk about the ick. Are you a twelve-year-old girl?"

The man on his left punched him in the back, but Darbo didn't collapse. He bit back the grunt of pain decided to recalculate his counterattack.

"You act as if I cheated," Darbo said.

"I don't know if you did or didn't," Garcha said. "I heard from a friend that you're a Darbinian. You didn't tell us your name was Darbinian. You gave us a *fake* name. You're related to Emin, right?"

Darbo's back still hurt where the other guy punched him. He answered through clenched teeth. "We're cousins."

"And you were sent here by your cousin, Emin, correct?"

"You owe him money."

Darbo grunted again as the short man jabbed the snout of the gun into his belly.

Cousin Emin was a big shot Armenian mobster; he controlled vice in a large portion of the country. Little worms like Sasoun Garcha were always a problem, always taking advantage, and Garcha had used up all the grace Cousin Emin was willing to give. As far as Cousin Emin was concerned, Garcha had pocketed the borrowed money and had no intention of paying it back. Cousin Emin asked Darbo, who happened to be between mercenary jobs, if he'd go and get the money. As a favor, of course. Darbo wasn't being paid for his time or soon, his trouble. Darbo couldn't help but note that every time he did a favor for Cousin Emin, he ended up fighting his way out of trouble.

"I owe him a bullet for sending one of his *thugs* to try and cheat at poker to *get* that money," the short man said.

"Nobody said I cheated, remember?"

Garcha took the gun away and his goons punched Darbo again, two solid blows to the back delivered at the same time. They also let go of him, and as Darbo started to fall to his knees while letting out a yell, he adjusted his footing and lunged at Garcha instead. The short man made the mistake of standing close to the poker table. Darbo collided with his midsection, forcing Garcha back into the table. They both landed on the table, and the legs buckled under their weight. Darbo and Garcha hit the floor hard but Garcha took the most punishment with Darbo's weight on top of him. The other two poker players bolted from the table. Cards and chips and bottles of beer splashed across the cement floor.

Darbo liked hearing the rush of air leaving Garcha's lungs, and his shocked expression of pain. Darbo liked even more that Garcha's gun flew from his grip on impact. The pistol skittered across the floor with the poker chips and stray cards. But Darbo was well aware there were still two goons on their feet and behind him, so he moved quick. Rolling off Garcha, he snatched a stray table leg off the floor and rolled some more, finally coming up on both feet with some distance between him and the two goons. The two tough guys closed the gap between them, and Darbo swung the thick wooden table leg. One *whack* to the side of the head and the first goon went down. The second managed to duck Darbo's swing, but had no way to dodge Darbo's follow-through kick, which forced the goon to double over, and then Darbo smashed him over the head with the table leg.

Garcha started the rise from the broken table. By the time he managed to prop himself up on one arm, Darbo had the short man's gun. Darbo stuck the snout of the gun in Garcha's left ear.

"I'm taking the bank, little man."

"This isn't over!"

"The hell it isn't." Darbo hit Garcha twice on the side of the head with the butt of the pistol.

The short man collapsed, unconscious, bleeding a little where the gun butt struck him, but Darbo didn't care. He stuck the gun in his belt and moved to another table near a wall. Garcha had placed the poker kit there, along with the little safe that held all the cash. Darbo took the small safe and held it tight as he walked up the steps of the basement to the house. The two poker players who'd fled the fight crouched low in a corner behind some stacked junk. Darbo shook his head at them and climbed the steps. He paused long enough at the basement door to take the gun out of his belt.

———————

AND DARBO WALKED out of the house without shooting, climbed into his car without harassment, and drove away with the safe full of cash resting on the passenger seat. He wasn't sure how much was in the safe, and he didn't care. One thing he knew for sure—

His phone rang.

Darbo took the cell from the hiding spot under the steering wheel and glanced at the readout. It was Lia! He answered.

"Yes, Lia, how are you?"

"Doing well. How about you?"

"I'm sore and angry and I'm never doing a favor for my cousin again!"

"But you're alive?"

"I love how you don't need to ask what I mean. Yes, I'm alive. You got work?"

"Big job, yes. Can you get to Oslo?"

"I'll be on the next flight out. After a bath and a big glass of gin."

"Make it vodka and I'll join you…in spirit."

Darbo laughed. "Send me details where to find you."

"On the way," she said.

ROGER JUSTICE WAS ON A MISSION. A mission for more beer.

Too much loafing around Virginia Beach, the city he called home, was dulling Roger's senses, and he felt the degrading effects of not being at war. There was only so much jogging one could do, and Roger had logged many laps around the beach in recent weeks. There was only so much bad TV and microwaved dinners one could consume. Despite his search for work, Roger hadn't had much luck getting out of the house for long periods of time. He was beginning to feel like the milk he usually left behind when he took a long-term assignment. Spoiled. He needed action and fast.

He walked from his apartment to the Liquor King a couple of blocks away. He wore a rock band T-shirt and faded jeans with a windbreaker. The ocean breeze brought chilly temperatures to the city, but the conditions were normal, and Roger didn't grumble about them. He waved at the counterman, Edward, an Iranian immigrant excited to take his citizenship test.

"Hello, Roger, my friend," Edward said as the door shut behind the mercenary. "My test is Wednesday at noon!"

"Good!"

"Ask me anything. *Anything*, I can answer."

"Who was the 18th president of the United States?" Roger asked him.

"General Grant," Edward said. "1869 to 1877."

"Was he a good president?"

"He was a big proponent of making Native Americans proper citizens." Edward beamed a big smile at Roger. He was short, pudgy, with gray hair and glasses perched on his nose. His yellow and black checkered shirt was unbuttoned at the top to expose graying chest hair.

"How ironic," Roger said, cutting away from the counter for the beer case.

"Are you out of beer again?"

"I'm always out of beer!" Roger called out. Navigating the crowded liquor store required careful steps. Racks jammed close together created narrow aisles, with additional merchandise stacked in unopened boxes. Edward might know his presidents and their accomplishments, but he wasn't much for neatness. Nobody within walking distance matched his stock, though. Edward had bottom-shelf and top-shelf liquor in various sized bottles; his beer selection was also extensive. Roger reached the beer section of the refrigerated aisle. Frost spotted the sliding doors behind which his elixir waited. He saw a case of Coors Banquet and decided what the heck. It wasn't fancy, but it wasn't terrible. As he slid open the door, the bell above the entrance chimed again. Edward let out a sharp cry of fear. Roger recognized the sound. He turned carefully and dropped low to get a better look. He peeked through openings in the display rack behind him.

"Time to open the register, old man."

Three of them. Male. Younger. Late teens, early twenties. The leader wore a black hoodie and carried a sawed-off shotgun. One of his buddies held a stainless steel revolver.

No Glocks? Roger thought. *Don't all these kids have Glocks today? What is this, discount Arms-R-Us?*

Edward lifted both hands to his shoulders, muttering, shaking, stepping back from the counter. He didn't have a lot of room. He almost bumped into the cigarette display behind him.

"You speak English?" the one with the shotgun demanded.

Edward stuttered but eventually said, "Yes."

"Then open it up and give us the cash. I'm not asking you again."

Roger's mind raced for a solution. He wasn't armed. He could take all three hand-to-hand, but not when two of them held firearms and looked dangerous enough to know how to make them go off. He didn't carry when not working, because there were laws against carrying concealed weapons without a license, and he didn't need the extra scrutiny of the law in his business. With crime as rampant as it had become in recent years, thanks to liberals who thought crooks had more rights than citizens, he decided society was falling into a terrible state indeed when one couldn't make a beer run without having to shoot it out with a trio of punks.

Roger moved left, farther down the aisle, as an idea popped into his mind. He had to make sure not to make any noise as he moved, and hoped Edward could stall the robbery crew long enough. He turned right into the next aisle ahead. Canned goods. A full can of anything made a perfect weapon if one could throw accurately.

Edward finally pressed the buttons to open the register and the kid with the shotgun told him to hurry. Roger found a can of Denison's Chili, a favorite, and held it tightly in his right hand. He moved forward. Carefully. Closer to the register. The punks would be on his left as he exited the aisle; he'd have concealment, but no cover. Any gunfire would blast through the store shelves and into him if he didn't score on the first throw.

One more step.

His right shoe squeaked against the polished tiled floor.

Aw, crap!

"Who's there?"

One of the kids turned to look. The one with the revolver. The third, not armed with a pistol, held a knife.

Roger threw the can hard. He'd have made a baseball scout proud. He didn't aim for the kids with the revolver or knife; he wanted the shotgunner first. The shotgunner was still focused on Edward and the pile of cash on the counter. The can bonked him on the side of the head. *Down goes Frasier!* The kid's legs buckled, and he collapsed against the counter, falling awkwardly to the floor. His body pinned the shotgun under him.

The other two, shocked by the sudden exit of their friend, gawked one second too long. Roger reached the kid with the revolver and twisted the kid's arm until it almost broke, forcing it behind the kid's back and bringing his body close as a shield against the one with the knife. Roger grabbed the revolver, bashed the second kid behind the ear, and stuck the gun in the third kid's face as his second buddy dropped to the floor.

"Drop the knife or I'll put one through your left eye."

The kid's hand opened, and the knife clattered at his feet. Roger didn't need to tell him to kick it away. He did so on his own, and the knife spun away.

"Call the police, Edward," Roger said. "Tell them we'll hold these three while they get their butts in gear."

Roger grinned. The kid holding his hands up whimpered. Liquor King might not be the kind of war zone he was used to, but Roger liked the rush fine enough.

THE POLICE SHOWED up fast enough, and in force. Four cars. Edward made sure to tell the 9-1-1 dispatcher there were multiple guns at the scene. Once the patrolmen understood Roger was the good guy, with Edward yelling that he had cameras to prove everything, they let him sit outside while they sorted the mess. Another officer took his account of what happened. When the officer excused himself to consult with a shift supervisor who also arrived, Roger sat on the sidewalk outside the store and let his mind wander. What a day. At least it was better than anything he had planned— which was nothing.

His cell phone rang. He pulled it from the inside pocket of his jacket and looked at the caller ID.

Lia Kenisova. He wondered what she wanted.

"Hi, Lia," he said.

"I need you in Oslo."

She's never been one for small talk, he thought. "For what?"

"Work, dummy. Are you free?"

Roger let out a satisfied breath. "Of course. Anything for you, darling."

"I need you here as soon as possible."

He looked around at the police officers; the patrol cars, haphazardly parked and taking up all the space in the parking lot; the passing traffic. It would be nice to get out of the chill, but what was he going into?

Who cared. It was action, and he needed action.

"I'm already halfway there," he said.

25

WAGNER AND GENEST, ALREADY IN OSLO, MOVED THROUGH A crowded warehouse with grim expressions. Genest was the most unhappy of the pair. He was about to lose a lot of money.

"We can't blow it up," he said to the German. "If the explosion ruptures the uranium container—"

"Yup," the German said. He looked around at the crates and heavy ordnance boxes stacked throughout the ground floor of the warehouse. The labels on the crates and containers betrayed nothing of what was within, but the number of weapons in one place astounded him. Small arms, explosives, heavy artillery, rockets. They had it all. Jet planes and helicopters and other transport vehicles were at different locations. Oslo is where they kept all the guns and bombs. The lights high above—they kept offices on the second floor—cast most of the lower section in shadows. They didn't want to advertise their presence too much, so Genest insisted on keepings the lights low.

Wagner said, "We never should have dealt ourselves into this, Roch."

"It sounded like a good idea at the time."

"Because we both had dollar signs in our eyes." The warehouse, like a lot of Oslo, bordered a waterway; he'd have been much happier sitting outside, watching the water and the boat traffic. But they had work to do first. If they were careful, he'd live long enough to watch water and boats for many years to come.

The pair started for the left side of the warehouse, stepping around crates and boxes to create their path.

"We'll forfeit the millions we paid."

"An expensive lesson," Wagner said.

"It's all so simple to you."

"Shouldn't it be? I hate to lose money too, but I'd like to keep breathing. We can't have both, Roch."

"What if we offered everything to La Bella? Wait for him to show up, and make sure the police are here when he does?"

"Best idea either of us have had all day," Wagner said.

They were visiting the warehouse at the perfect time of night, after midnight, when there was no traffic on the street and other businesses around them were closed. Boat traffic didn't bother either of them. None of the traffic in the harbor would have a good view of what happened on land. Genest had made sure to stack dilapidated construction equipment in the back to create a barrier between the warehouse and the waterway. The outside of the warehouse made it look like their business was reconditioning construction vehicles. It was nice and benign for almost a decade and now a little punk trying to become Carlos the Jackal threatened everything.

"We spent a lot of money to get all this," Wagner said. "We can afford to lose a little."

"It's more than a little!" Genest said.

"We can make up the difference. All our other items are steady sellers. I have an order pending for the X-17 missiles we picked up two years ago."

"How many?"

"All of them, plus the launchers."

"Well, that's good, at least. You probably have a point. Best to let it go. Nothing here is under our names, and we can clear it out fast enough."

"If we try to hold out, it will only end badly."

"I know. But it was—"

"Shut up already, Roch." Wagner and Genest stopped in front of an addition built inside the warehouse, a box with steel walls. He used a key to unlatch the also-made-of-steel door, then punched a code into a number pad. Three other locks clicked back, and Wagner eased the door open. There wasn't much inside. Ten items sat near a corner. One looked like a large cylindrical garbage can, lead-lined, with heavy foam padding creating a narrow tunnel down the center. Three items were encased in stainless steel, one with exposed circuitry on one end. Two of the smaller stainless steel cylinders may have been tall cans of food, neither without a label.

They were the disassembled parts of the Soviet-era back-pack nuclear weapon. The United States and NATO version bore the named Special Atomic Demolition Munition. Genest didn't care what the Russians called it; the name must have been spelled out in the Cyrillic lettering on the casing that resembled a garbage can. All he knew was the weapon, fully assembled, was useless. The battery was dead, nothing but a large paperweight. The older battery tech had been long abandoned; refreshing or rebuilding it wasn't an option. The only way to make money on the weapon was to sell the parts, and reverse engineer the most valuable piece of equipment in the case: the trigger mechanism. The rest? They didn't know what to do with the rest. The uranium in the larger of the two stainless cylinders could fetch a high price, but it was easier to keep it hidden, out of the way, and make money on the trigger pieces.

At least it was, until hell broke loose.

"All right, here's what we do." Genest turned to face the rest of the warehouse. "Clear everything out. Should take a couple of days, but I think we have the time. Then, we tell the authorities the nuke is here, and they need to dispose of it. They'll spend months trying to track us, but the shell companies and cut-outs this warehouse relates to should keep them busy long enough for us to get clear. What do you think?"

"I think—"

Wagner stopped and drew his gun.

Genest heard the noise too. A clang of metal on metal. He drew his own gun and turned to Wagner. Combat was the younger man's game, and Wagner gestured ahead to a cluster of crates bathed in shadow.

But Genest still knew a thing or two about fighting. Whoever was knocking on the door would get one heck of a lesson.

___

CASSIANO LA BELLA wondered if a water approach would have been better, but it was too late to change. Simona drove the black SUV along the street leading to Genest's warehouse, and they were minutes away.

"Check your weapons."

The order didn't come from Cassiano, but from Jack Moss in the back seat with Sergio. Moss supplied the guns, battered but functional H&K MP5SD3 9mm submachine guns. It was the version of the MP-5 with the integral suppressor; the barrel looked thicker than usual, but most of the exterior circumference came from the built-in suppressor. The weapons were almost whisper quiet, except for the cycling of the action. They needed the silence in case of shooting, and Cassiano intended to do some shooting. Sergio had trailed Genest and Wagner from an office building to the warehouse. They knew the arms dealers were inside.

Oslo wasn't the last stop. Moss's intelligence was clear. The nuclear trigger circuits were not inside the warehouse, but at another location, as yet undetermined. They needed to get the information out of Wagner or the Frenchman and go find more triggers. The Frenchman and German being dead was a bonus, and Cassiano wanted to blow the warehouse, too. Burn it down with well-placed C4 charges. Let the uranium in the Soviet backpack nuke loose on the population, a glorious statement of his arrival. He hated he couldn't take immediate credit, but once they were in the United States with the completed bomb, he'd have a chance to make his actions known. He'd let the world know he wasn't to be treated as anything less than the most dangerous terrorist alive.

But Moss nixed the idea.

Cassiano, in the front seat beside Simona, checked his H&K by feel. The bolt was closed, and they'd entered the SUV with empty chambers. The interior filled with the *clack-clack* of Cassiano and Sergi charging their weapons. Cassiano clicked on his safety too. Jack Moss, armed only with a handgun, checked his pistol. Simona, driving, did not. She rounded another curve and shut off the headlights. The warehouse loomed ahead.

Simona eased the car to the curb before the warehouse's driveway. She was out first, grabbing her H&K from where she'd stowed it, racking the charging handle. By the time she took up position at the front fender, watching, Cassiano and the others exited. Moss turned to Sergio.

"You're sure they're alone?"

"It was only the two of them," Sergio said.

"We don't need any surprises," Cassiano said.

"There won't be."

Cassiano didn't like the blaring street lamps, but there was nothing to do short of shooting them out. The lights might expose them on their approach, but then he took in the parking lot. There were plenty of derelict construction vehicles to use as cover. They could approach the front without being seen, as long as the German and the Frenchman weren't looking out the windows. He didn't think they would be.

Moss took the lead. Cassiano followed behind, but not too close. It was best to maintain distance between the soldier ahead of you so one bullet didn't go through two. Simona ran beside him, with Sergio in the rear. Moss led them across the lot to a tractor; they spread out to examine the area once again, each taking a different angle. Cassiano saw nothing alarming. No sentries. The front of the warehouse was shrouded in shadows, and he had no way to see if there were any cameras out front. He figured there had to be. Perhaps, even, an infrared sensor to set off an alarm once they crossed the beam. Despite the chilly night, he felt sweat down his back.

There was no turning back. He'd crossed the point of no return long ago, Simona pledging to follow. No matter the risks, they had to go forward. His future—his and Simona's—depended on their success.

Moss made a forward gesture with his right hand, and they resumed the approach.

A SMALL BLACKED-OUT speed boat sliced through the waterway on its way to the warehouse. The three people aboard gave passing glances to other docks and structures along the way, but the warehouse was the only destination they had in mind.

Roger Justice sat at the wheel, keeping to the right to avoid other traffic. Most were larger, shipping vessels making late runs to other docks amid the many waterways in Oslo. Over his right shoulder stood Lia Kenisova, and Roger tried not to think of her as a backseat driver. But the Russian beauty liked to micro-manage, have a hand in every decision; she was the opposite of Sam Raven, and Roger would have preferred having his old buddy in charge. A job was a job, though, and it beat the hell out of jogging on Virginia Beach.

Roger and Darbo had asked about Raven when they met Lia is Oslo, but her answer had been brief and to the point.

"He's probably busy."

"We should call him anyway," Darbo suggested.

"You want to go home?"

Darbo said no. They continued the mission without Raven.

Dressed in black and loaded for war, the trio had one goal in mind. Capture either Wagner or Genest and take them to a secure location for a chat about nuclear parts. Lia had her country's honor at stake; Roger and Darbo had a paycheck at stake. But they liked Lia, so they wanted her to succeed. She'd be unbearable if they failed and yell a lot. Nobody wanted to be around Lia when she was yelling. It was even worse if she was drunk, and if they failed, she'd be very drunk. It was important they didn't fail so she didn't get drunk and start yelling.

But going into a potential firefight cold wasn't anybody's idea of a good time.

They had to overwhelm the enemy before they had a chance to shoot back.

"Can you go faster?" Lia said.

"You want the harbor patrol to stop us?" Roger asked. "We have speed limits on the water too."

"A little faster."

Roger shook his head. He pushed forward on the throttle —but only a little.

26

MOSS REACHED THE WALL OF THE WAREHOUSE FIRST. THEY didn't want to go through the front door, which led to a lobby and some offices; the side door offered the access they wanted. But the side door also had the toughest lock. The four of them stayed in the shadows as they followed the wall to a corner. Moss moved around first, where he stopped at a chain-link fence. He used a pair of strong wire cutters to snip the links. Each link snapped as the cutters bit; the sound was too loud for Cassiano, who stayed around the corner and watched. But Moss moved swiftly and soon created an opening. Moss held the broken links to the side while Cassiano, Simona, and Sergio crawled through, then he followed after easing the gap closed once again. The others fanned out, weapons up, while he came through, and one by one followed in his wake as he approached one of the side doors.

Cassiano turned his attention toward the back end of the warehouse. The dock stretching into the waterway looked black under the night sky, but Oslo beyond was brightly lit, the city still active even at the late hour. He watched Moss at the door. Moss examined the lock, an electronic panel/dead bolt combination. He used a traditional set of lock picks on the dead bolt, but the electrical panel needed another tool. Moss used a small unit the size of a TV remote, but with a magnetic strip extending from the top. A set of small screws secured a cover plate to the bottom of the panel, and he removed the screws and the panel, revealing a slot. Moss inserted the end of the strip into the slot and the device in his hand came to life, lighting up. Cassiano would have loved a lesson on the equipment, an explanation of how it worked, but now wasn't the time for such questions.

Moss worked in silence while Cassiano, Simona, and Sergio kept watch. Cassiano perked up every time a boat sailed past the dock; they weren't the only ones interested in Genest and Wagner's secrets. Sam Raven was still on his mind, too. The American wasn't stupid. Despite Moss's promise to the contrary, and the suggestion Raven had only Berlin as his next lead, Cassiano knew Raven would learn about Oslo somehow. He might even be on one of the passing boats looking for an opportunity to visit.

Focus. You're looking for a boogeyman under your bed.

Back to Moss again. The older man removed the magnetic strip and punched in a set of numbers. A light on the panel turned from red to green and he waved them toward him. By the time Cassiano joined the others, Moss was holding the door—

Clang.

With the H&K out in front of him, Cassiano started through the doorway, only to bang the snout of the MP5SD3 on the doorframe. He didn't need to see the reactions of his compatriots; there was nothing to do except continue. Moss pulled the door shut, and they crouched within to listen for any sign of somebody alerted to their entry.

They must have heard, Cassiano thought.

Unless the warehouse was empty and their visit for naught...

WAGNER, behind a crate with pistol in hand, knew better than to try and see in the low light. Listening was his best weapon now, and despite his rapid pulse, he didn't hear any footsteps or any other sounds indicating the presence of others. No alarm sounded; he and Genest had disabled the system when they arrived.

"It's Cassiano," Genest said.

Wagner's eyes probed the darkness while he listened. Then, a small sound. A quick click. If he hadn't been listening, he would have missed the noise and not recognized the significance. It was the click of somebody turning on a flashlight, and Wagner held a finger to his lips to keep Genest from saying more. They both watched the beam of the flashlight shine up one wall to the steps leading to the second-level offices, and the walkway overlooking the warehouse floor.

The light snapped off.

"They're trying to see if we're here," Genest said. "How many, do you think?"

"Who cares? We have a warehouse full of weapons. Come on. Got a plan."

Wagner pivoted and started at a crouch away from the crate. He didn't look back to see if Genest followed, but knew he'd be there. He straightened once the crates became taller, then took a knee at a stack of smaller wooden boxes. The boxes were elongated wooden cases, and Wagner lifted a lid to one. Hand grenades sat like a carton of eggs within the box, and the German selected a smoke grenade. He put his gun away, pulled the pin, and gestured for Genest to follow him. He kept a tight grip on the grenade as he advanced.

CASSIANO LEFT his position to approach Moss, who was waving his damn flashlight around. Cassiano touched the older man's shoulder and kneeled beside him to whisper, "What the hell are you doing, Jack?"

"Are they here or not?" Moss cut off the light. "If not, we need to get up to those offices and see what's there."

Sergio came over. "I was watching till you guys picked me up. They didn't leave."

"They didn't leave from an exit you could see," Moss said.

"They didn't leave at all," Cassiano insisted, "and you just showed them where we are."

"I'm not the one who bashed his gun on the door."

Simona cursed and started moving, passing the three arguing men to step further into the maze of crates. Cassiano left them to keep up with her. *All right, second floor is the goal till further notice…*

27

WAGNER AND GENEST MOVED THROUGH THE CRATE MAZE WITH Genest breathing harder than Wagner would have liked. If they survived, he'd recommend the boss go to work busting the bowling ball belly under his shirt.

The stairs to the second level were his goal. If the intruders thought it was important to get up there, he'd meet them with an ambush. A smoke charge and rapid-fire pistol shots would do the job, but the smoke grenade was a double-edged sword. The only vents in the warehouse were in the roof, and the giant fans hanging above to help with air circulation weren't on. He and Genest would feel the effects of the smoke, too. Choking. Watery eyes. But they'd have to push through to win.

Wagner dropped flat on the hard floor as shooting started. Genest landed beside him, almost winded by their fast pace. The *phuts* of automatic gunfire and the clicking of actions told Wagner a lot. Cassiano and his people carried suppressed submachine guns. And the shots weren't aimed at him and Genest. They were aimed at the lights. Fluorescent bulbs popped and snapped; the metal beams holding the bulbs screeched as bullets tore through. The lights winked out, plunging the interior from near darkness to total darkness.

Great, blind and stuck in a maze...

But no lights made Cassiano's crew bold. They moved faster, their footsteps scraping the floor, the beam of a flashlight glowing among the crates. Somebody bumped into a crate anyway and yelled. A woman. Cassiano's girlfriend and —who else? There were too many footsteps for only two people.

"Enough waiting," Genest hissed, and rose high enough to start firing. His gun was loud in the large, but confined, space. Wagner turned away so his vision wasn't hurt by the flashing muzzle of Genest's handgun. The Frenchman triggered four quick shots from his large-capacity 9mm, shifting his aim with each pull of the trigger. He ducked again. At least one round whined off the concrete wall near the steps. The others? Since nobody screamed, Wagner hoped the boss wasn't doing too much damage to the merchandise. But it was a lousy time to worry about money, considering their earlier argument...

"Come on," Wagner snapped. He and Genest left their position. Return fire came immediately. Cassiano had a fix on their spot because of the muzzle flashes; but as Wagner poked his head up for a peek, he saw the other side didn't offer the same courtesy. The flashlight was out, and their submachines guns were not only suppressed, but had flash hiders too.

Wagner held out his free hand, not the one holding the grenade, to avoid crashing into a crate. He stopped and dropped. The shooting and associated noise was ahead and to the right, but his vision only allowed him to see vague outlines. He threw the smoke grenade. Genest fired twice. He was wasting ammo shooting at shadows, but Wagner wasn't going to correct the boss in the middle of a fight.

The grenade *thunk-thunked* against obstacles, then clattered and spun across the floor. Somebody yelled. Wagner fired once round in the direction of the yell.

SERGIO, Cassiano's gunman, knew the sound of a grenade. The explosive bounced off a nearby crate and hit the floor and slid toward him. He yelled and kicked out, hoping to connect despite not seeing it; his foot struck something, and sent the grenade sliding across the floor in another direction.

A shot aimed at him *chunked* into the top edge of a crate. He dropped and rolled away, but there were no other shots. The grenade popped. Instead of an explosion of shrapnel, a hiss of thick smoke filled the warehouse. The cloud grew steadily. Sergio stayed low. The crates altered the course of the smoke this way and that, but he felt the sting in his eyes right away. He coughed a little. Covering his face, he kept his head to the cement.

They'd face a stalemate and a swarm of Oslo cops if they didn't bring the fight to an end. They were like submarines deep in the ocean, each probing for the other in a cat-and-mouse exercise, but they had to bring it to a close. *Fast.*

Sergio broke left. He wanted to find and disable Genest and Wagner. Cassiano shouted at him, but he ignored the command. Let the other three approach the objective. Moss thought information of value waited above—in one of the offices. Sergio wasn't as sure. Better to get what they wanted from the source as specified in their original plan.

At least he knew he hadn't made a mistake.

Genest and Wagner were still in the building.

———

FANS. They needed the fans!

Cassiano and Simona stayed flat, both wiping their eyes with one hand to keep the other on their weapons. But what good were weapons when you couldn't see? Moss said he'd find the control panel for the fans. It had to be somewhere on the first floor—probably along the wall. All they had to do was hold on a little longer. Cassiano saw Sergio moving away and yelled his name, but the gunman ignored the order and went his own way. *He's going to try to flank Genest!* But Sergio could possibly send fire in *their* direction, so he eased Simona up and they moved toward the wall. Once the smoke cleared…

But he didn't want to think so far ahead. Not when the enemy was still sniping at them.

They took refuge once more behind a tall crate. How much money did Genest have in the warehouse? Blowing it up now seemed like a waste. Taking over for the arms-dealing Frenchman could fund countless operations and training camp sessions…

It can't be all about destruction, right?

But it had to be, this time. Next time? Maybe he'd apply the lessons learned.

Or maybe he wouldn't.

The nice thing about being the best was you could pick and choose which lessons you wanted to follow and when.

———

"NOW WE GO HUNTING," Wagner said.

"I'm not crawling on the floor like a bug, not in this smoke."

Somebody coughed and made a choking noise. It was someone close who had a slap of the smoke across the face. Wagner turned in time to see Sergio come around a crate and bring up his H&K. Wagner yelled for Genest to move, but the overweight Frenchman did so too slowly. Wagner, on his feet, pistol in a two-hand grip, covered two steps in a flash, and positioned himself between Genest and Sergio. Both men fired at the same time. Wagner's pistol barked and kicked; his shots cored through Sergio's chest with two wet slaps, the last sounds Sergio ever heard before the lights went out forever. But Sergio's suppressed triple-burst of 9mm slugs did likewise to his opponent, stitching Wagner chest to throat and punching out through his back. Both collapsed on the concrete floor. Wagner let out a choked rattle and then went silent and still. His body lay limp, his eyeglasses askew.

Genest stared in shock at Wagner's dead body. There was nothing he could do for his old friend, so he scrambled over Wagner's body to the other dead man and helped himself to Sergio's weapon and spare magazines. He was breathing hard, feeling dizzy, his eyes watery; he wiped his eyes, then stuffed magazines in the pockets of his trousers. He didn't need to see the weapon to know what it was, a Heckler & Koch MP5SD3. He'd sold thousands of them over the years and knew the SMG backward and forward.

He stood up and yelled, "We killed your man! Now we're coming for you!"

And the French Foreign Legion veteran started hunting. He wasn't in the best shape, yeah; but fury had a way of making up the difference. He wasn't winded or tired or sore any longer. He was out to avenge his fallen comrade, and nobody was going to get in his way.

Genest stopped and took a knee as another sound joined the echo of gunfire. The rumble of small motors, then a breeze. The fans above were turning, picking up speed, soon to suck the smoke out of the warehouse. Genset wished he could get some lights on, but no matter. You play the hand you're dealt. He moved out with the H&K in the ready position.

Ready to kill.

28

CASSIANO HEARD THE WORDS AND SPRANG TO HIS FEET. Simona tried to grab him, but he moved too fast for her, running through the maze, looking for Genest. The fans were running at full speed, sucking out the smoke; his eyes watered a little, but not enough to slow him down. He dodged around the crates, H&K up and searching, conscious of Simona yelling for him to come back. No. He wasn't going back. Sergio was the last—all of his men were gone, men who'd pledged their lives to the cause and to him. He was tired of leaving their deaths unavenged. First, Genest. Then, Raven.

"Come out, old man!"

Cassiano swung left, right, shifted around a crate; nothing. He pivoted, sensing movement, and spotted Genest bracing his stolen weapon. Cassiano fired, showering the Frenchman's face with wood chips as the burst chewed into the crate; Genest fired back, two quick shots, but Cassiano was already rolling across the floor, using the limited space to his advantage. Up, firing again, Genest moving out of the way, surprisingly spry for a fat man, or perhaps it was only his imagination. Cassiano pressed forward, moving erratically, ducking, rising, looking for a shot. A rush of footsteps behind him. He spun, but held his fire when Simona emerged.

"We do this together or not at all," she said.

The pair moved forward, scanning for their quarry.

"Where are you, old man?" Cassiano yelled.

It was as if Genest has disappeared...

Jack Moss didn't feel a moment of sorrow for poor Sergio.

With Cassiano and Simona tied up with Roch Genest, Moss took the opportunity to race headlong for the stairs. They were metal steps, and his boots clanged loudly as he took the first few. He moved as fast as he could while scanning for Genest at the same time. He and the Frenchman spotted each other. Moss fired, Genest fired; both missed, with Moss feeling the light shock of the rounds striking the concrete wall on his right. He yelled to Cassiano, trying to tell him Genest's position, but the Frenchman was on the move again. Moss fired at him, striking the ground, then continued upward. The pair of offices at the top, with the walkway in front of them, would give him another perch to fight from. The Frenchman had no chance. But he hoped the clues leading to the location of the nuclear triggers waited within the office. Somewhere. Perhaps on a computer or a notebook.

More gunfire below. Moss used it to his advantage and climbed faster.

Reaching the top landing, he looked for Genest, didn't see him, and charged through the doorway of the first office. Let Cassiano and Simona do the hard work. He had to hurry to complete his part. Searching the offices was his idea, after all.

CASSIANO AND SIMONA traded shots with Genest, the Frenchman ducking away, his footsteps scraping against the concrete floor. Cassiano kneeled to reload while Simona covered him. She breathed hard while he ejected one magazine, let it fall, and grabbed another from his carry pouch. Simona's head turned left, right; Genset was somewhere within the mass of crates. He'd pop out like a rattlesnake if they let their guard down for one moment. The magazine clicked into place, Cassiano rose to full height—

"Down!"

He shoved Simona out of the way with his left arm and fired the MP5SD3, the ejecting shell casings tinkling onto the floor. Genest emerged from between two crates, lining up both in his sights, but Cassiano's burst shredded open the Frenchman's chest and sent him sprawling.

Cassinao, breathing hard, stared at the fallen body. *No. We needed him alive!*

Simona stood, and he turned to her, eyes wide, mouth open. She looked at the dead man and turned back to him.

"You stupid—"

Cassiano's face tightened in anger. "It was you or him, baby."

"Stop arguing!"

They pivoted to the sound of Moss's voice. He stood on the walkway in front of the offices, holding up the backpack he'd strapped to his back at the beginning of the fight. "We got what we need!"

"We can't leave Sergio," Cassiano said.

Moss was halfway down the steps, rushing as fast as he could without falling. "Sorry, kid. No room for the dead."

Cassiano wanted to argue, but as Moss reached the

ground floor and ran through the maze to them, Simona grabbed his arm. He snapped his attention to her.

"He's right."

Cassiano sighed. "All right."

"Come on, kids," Moss said. He breezed past them heading for the side door they'd entered from.

———————————

"THERE'S THE DOCK!" Lia Kenisova shouted over the grumble of the speedboat's engine.

"I see it," Roger told her. He didn't bother to raise his voice. There was no need. They all knew what they were looking at, and they all knew what they had to do.

But Lia gave the orders anyway. "Ruck up and prepare for landing!"

Roger remained at the controls, not bothering with his gear, but Lia and Darbo hurried into their combat rigs and checked their SIG SG-552 Commando automatic rifles. Roger slowed the boat, steering for the dock, and eased the craft alongside. He tossed a line, jumped out, and twisted the line around a hook on the edge of the dock. Darbo and Lia climbed onto the dock while Roger grabbed his rifle. Lia took the lead. They had a 25-yard dash from the dock to the rear area of the warehouse, and the derelict construction equipment loomed large and imposing in the dark. A few light posts burned bright, but not enough—which was a good thing for combat, bad for finding their way in an unfamiliar place.

They weren't even sure if Genset and Wagner would be at the warehouse at this time of night, but Lia was counting on discovering the stash of nuclear triggers and what remained of the Soviet backpack nuke. She wanted to secure the nuke parts and drop a dime to an FSB unit nearby, one waiting for her call. They'd come and collect the nuclear parts. She and Darbo would gather any intel laying around that might lead them to more of Genest and Wagner's stashes of weapons, in case they missed the prize and needed to look elsewhere. But Lia felt confident what they needed was within the warehouse.

Clearing the junkyard, they waited at the edge of the pavement before stepping into open ground. The back wall of the warehouse was ten yards away. The open space of concrete was the wavy, textured type. A bitch to fall on. But no guards. No cameras were pointed in their direction. Lia frowned.

She said to Roger, "You'd think there would be more security."

"Not if they want a low profile," the American mercenary said.

Darbo scanned the area through an infrared scope. He lowered the unit and said, "No cameras, no invisible beams to trip over."

"We go?" she said.

"I say we go."

Lia leaped to her feet and started at a quick pace. She reached the door first, Roger and Darbo behind her. The only doors on the back wall were large sliding doors going from ground to roof; for loading and unloading the big stuff. They weren't about to mess with those doors. Inching around the corner, Lia took a knee and peered around. Open ground, chain-link fence blocking the way to the front. No sign of activity. She gestured for Roger and Darbo to follow her, and they rounded the corner.

A side door ahead swung open. Nobody at the door paid attention to silence. They were in a hurry. Lia counted three, two men and a woman, racing to the fence. One carried a full backpack on his back; their H&K submachine guns were also plainly visible. Lia stopped short, but they heard her skid. The woman looked back and shouted an alarm, spinning around, still moving backward as she let rip with a burst from her weapon.

Lia hit the ground first, Roger and Darbo rolling away as the salvo smacked into the side of the warehouse. She jammed her SG-552 into her shoulder and fired back, one shot, but the woman was already running, and her companions unleashed more fire as they reached the fence. Lia fired back and moved to the corner again, grateful for the lack of outside lights. The shadows concealed her, but they wouldn't stop a bullet should one find its mark. She scooted around the corner. Darbo and Roger had run for cover elsewhere; she couldn't see where they'd gone, but they weren't lying in the open.

What the hell was going on?

Duh, somebody's shooting at you.

Why?

They're here for the same thing you are!

Lia swung around the corner, but the trio was already through the hole in the fence and running around the front of the warehouse. Roger broke cover and ran for the fence, Lia following, Darbo appearing beside her. By the time they reached the chain link, the SUV the other trio arrived in was screeching into the street, leaving behind a trail of tire smoke.

"I have a bad feeling about this," Roger said.

"A quick look inside won't hurt," Lia said. She started back for the warehouse.

"The hell it won't," Roger called after her.

"Come on," Darbo said, following Lia. "You know how she is."

"I certainly do."

Roger joined his friend.

With flashlights, they found the bodies and the spent shell casings and eventually the leftover Soviet nuke parts. Breaking into the steel room required Darbo's skill and some of his electronic lock-breaking equipment. Lia at least had a job for the FSB unit in Oslo, but otherwise the effort was a dead end. Whoever they traded shots with reached the prize first.

29

RAVEN HAD ONE QUESTION FOR TRACY:

"What do we know?"

They were in their hotel room in Berlin, having spent the last few days on surveillance. Raven stood in front of a whiteboard with a red pen, Tracy sat at in a corner chair.

"Ernesto Montego leaves his home about eight forty-five every morning and spends the day at the Free University of Berlin." She read from a notebook. Raven made notes on a whiteboard, the tip of the red pen squeaking on the surface of the board. "He eats lunch at the university cafeteria, holds court with students, continues his lectures; he leaves promptly at six o'clock every night and goes home to his wife. Lights out for both of them at ten every night. No deviation on this routine for the last couple of days."

Raven capped the pen. The lights were on in the room, the drapes closed. Raven wished he could have opened the window to let in the sounds of the city, but as usual, the windows didn't unlatch.

"No outside activity," Raven said. "No nights out with the wife. No coffee with friends."

"These aren't the habits of a terrorist mastermind."

Raven examined a tablet on a table in front of him and scrolled through the series of pictures they took of Montego going about his business. Tracy was right. No activity other than his daily routine; no meeting in smoke-filled rooms to plot dastardly deeds. The pictures of Montego showed an elderly man who wore an old man's clothes and blended in with the rest of the population. Nothing about him stood out. If he'd once been a charismatic Latin American terrorist leader, now he looked like Grandpa. The top of his head was bare; tufts of hair sat above his ears and crawled around the back of his head.

"He might be La Bella's teacher," Raven said, "but I think he's quit the field. Prison changed him."

"He wrote a book, remember? After he got out of prison. He wrote about his life and went on a repentance tour. You can look it up. Some of his TV appearances are online and there are plenty of newspaper articles, too. The university decided to offer him a job, and the vote wasn't even close. They sent him packing the first time. After a while, they proposed the idea again, and the second time they voted to hire him."

"Because why? Why the change of heart?"

"He'd formed the Council for Economic Equality, started publishing, and hosted lectures. He's never run from his past, but he's always referring to his change of heart. He'd rather publish and speak than participate in murder and mayhem."

Raven set the tablet down and examined the notes on the whiteboard. "No evidence the council supports terrorism. Nothing we dug up about them is dirty."

"What if Montego isn't the connection we're looking for?"

"Somebody else in the council?"

"Makes sense, right?"

"A cadre of the council reviving Montego's violent past without his knowledge? I suppose."

"Too bad we can't audit the council's money. See how they're using their funds?"

"Uh-huh."

"What do you think?"

"I think we should go have a chat with Mr. Montego and see what he says."

"We'll find out the truth one way or another," Tracy said.

———

WATCHING his students leave was always the toughest part of every lecture period.

Figuring out why took a bit of time for Ernesto Montego, but he sorted out the reasons soon enough. During a lecture, he was engaged, focused, and feeling the energy from his audience of students as they listened, took notes, asked questions, and helped him create a conversation about the issues he lectured on. His classes weren't for only him to talk and tell the students what they should consider and think. He wanted a two-way conversation. He wanted to keep them engaged. Some, of course, opposed his ideas; he welcomed the debate. A civil disagreement didn't bother him, but he was always on the alert for when the discussion became hostile.

But when the lecture was over, when the class session ended, and the students gathered their notes and papers and departed for the next stop on their agendas, Montego had to turn off. He didn't want to stop, but it wasn't productive to talk to a room full of empty chairs unless you wanted a trip to the funny farm. There were plenty of people who wanted to see him locked up forever, anyway. Why give them further reasons? It was in the process of turning off where he felt drained, alone, and a little sad. The high was gone.

The door to his classroom shut as the last student left. He didn't have another class until after lunch, and his wife had packed his sandwich and fruit for the day so there'd be no buying a hot sandwich at the cafeteria this afternoon. He still planned to go there to eat, though. The cafeteria was always loud, full of people, and a nice place to sit and be alone without submitting to silence. Montego didn't like silence. He didn't like the way his mind wandered during periods of quiet, wandered to the dark places. He'd committed to never going back to those places again, and it took the commitment as seriously as his wedding vows.

He tried to convince his students that his past life was a mistake, he'd paid a price for it, and they should avoid making similar choices. Some ignored his wisdom. He didn't know what to do about them, because he had no true knowledge of their activity, and only suspicions about who was involved.

He sat behind his desk and began making changes to the day's lesson plan and adjusting his lecture notes based on earlier questions. The only sound in the room, other than his breathing, was the light tap of his fingers on a laptop keyboard. He was so focused on the glowing screen and the words displayed he didn't hear his classroom door open. But he heard the footsteps of the man who entered.

Montego looked up.

"You aren't a student," he said, making sure to sound friendly. Because a chill crept up his neck. The man wore casual clothes and a jacket, but the clothing couldn't disguise the trim physique and sharp eyes. The man was a hunter.

"I'm not," said Sam Raven.

30

"I AM AT A DISADVANTAGE THEN, SIR," MONTEGO SAID.

Montego was sharp. He sized up Raven the same way Raven sized him up. They were both warriors, one active, one retired, but the base instincts never left. Montego knew exactly what Raven was, but not who. The who didn't matter, really. Raven was simply another agent of the "authorities" whom Montego had dealt with many times throughout his life.

"I'm Sam Raven."

"You're American?"

"Yes."

"I appreciate you haven't tried to pass yourself off as a reporter or a member of another benign profession."

"We talked about it," Raven said.

"We?"

"I'm not alone. My associate is waiting to hear from me."

Montego smiled. It was a small, ironic smile.

"I know why you're here," the teacher said. "Why don't you have a seat, and we'll talk."

Raven stepped further into the classroom as Montego grabbed a student chair and positioned it in front of his desk. He moved fast and wasn't concerned with turning his back to his visitor. Raven looked around. It had been many years since he'd visited a classroom of any type, but they always looked the same. Tiled floor, stained here and there after thousands of steps. Walls bearing images of socialist leaders of the past. Soviet, Latin American, Asian—Raven recognized the faces, knew the names, the history, and had to take a deep breath. Now wasn't the time for political arguments or inflammatory statements. He had a goal, he needed information, he required Montego's cooperation. But Raven did not sit. He wanted the professor to know while the visit wasn't hostile, there'd only be the suggestion of a truce. Montego sat behind his desk again and didn't ask Raven to sit a second time.

"You're here because some of my students have made poor choices, aren't you?"

"You're aware?" Raven said.

"I know there are a few trying to take after my old life, the life I told them to avoid, but when you're a proponent of alternative forms of government and economics—"

Raven tried not to laugh, but he supposed the old man was right. Marxist socialism *was* an alternative to capitalism, but he wasn't used to hearing it spoken about in vague terms that made it sound like choosing between hot tea and iced tea.

"—certain true believers come to see only one way to implement those alternatives. With bombs and bullets. No matter how much I preach against violence, it still has an allure to some. And those students have taken it upon themselves to learn the violent ways."

"And you let it happen."

"A statement instead of a question, Mr. Raven?"

"If you knew what they were doing, why didn't you alert authorities?"

"I had no proof, no knowledge. If you're here to see me, it means something *has* happened, has it not? Or one of them has been caught with a bomb? I can give you a list of names, students who've dropped my class, but I know not all of them have gone and done something illegal."

"Cassiano La Bella."

A shadow crossed Montego's face. "Oh, no."

Raven gave the professor a rundown of the last few days. He wasn't obliged to keep secrets for the CIA or anybody else, and didn't hold back. He wanted to shock Montego with as much data as possible, as much *damning* information as possible, regarding his former students. He even took out his phone in the middle of his explanation and read the names of the dead in Tangier. The ones he'd encountered at the Airbnb and killed, although he didn't tell Montego he was the one who ended their lives. With each nugget of information, a weight landed on Montego's shoulders. He slumped in his chair and his facial expressions were those of a man beaten; betrayed; a man shocked into silence. It was one thing to suspect, another to know.

When Raven finished, he let the silence fill the room a moment. Montego stared at his desktop in a daze.

"He promised me…"

"Who?"

"Cassiano. To my face. He promised he'd never go and do what I did. I thought I'd reached him."

"What happened between you and him?"

Montego leaned back in his chair. The chair looked well-worn, and it squeaked. The teacher looked hurt. He was taking Raven's words personally. This wasn't how Raven expected the conversation to go, and he didn't interrupt Montego as he continued.

"He read my book. Most of my students do. But Cassiano agreed with my twenty-year-old self, the one who said the only way to make society change was by force. He comes from a rich family. He never lacked anything, and he saw the less fortunate as victims of a society favoring the rich. He wanted to cut *down* the rich, make them as low as the have-nots. He had a real zeal. Real *anger*. Like a personal vendetta against his father or whoever, I had no idea, but it wasn't uncommon to see even back in my day. Those are the ones who flamed out the fastest and usually took people with them."

"All he did was read your book?" Raven asked.

"No, he read others. We talked about those, too. I did everything I could to steer him away, but he and several others soon dropped out of the university and vanished. Nobody knew where they'd gone, but I had an idea."

"What was your idea?"

"They found a connection. I have no idea how, but somebody found them, or they found somebody, and wound up at a training camp in the Middle East or Africa, same as I did. It isn't—tough to do, if you look hard enough. They probably did it through some online forum."

"Who did they find, Professor? If it wasn't you, it has to be somebody close to you. Somebody who works for your council, maybe?"

Montego closed his eyes. "I pray not."

"Your wishes aren't good enough," Raven said. "Right now, you're lucky it's only me talking to you. We still have time to stop La Bella and what's left of his crew."

"I can't help you."

"Who are your closest associates at the council?"

"You want me to betray—"

"Yeah," Raven said. "I want you to inform on your friends. One of them is guilty. One of them not only knows what La Bella is doing, he knows who's paying for it. He or she may even be using council funds to make it all happen. If your little organization is connected to a terrorist incident, everything you've worked for will be destroyed. Are you prepared for that? I don't agree with anything you teach, but if you're innocent in all of this, you don't deserve to be taken down because of what your students have done."

Montego didn't look at Raven, but past him, at the seats his students occupied. Raven wondered what he was thinking.

"You have to let me…" Montego trailed off. He cleared his throat.

"Let you do what?" Raven said.

Montego looked at Raven. The hurt was gone, replaced with resolve. There was fire, again, behind his eyes. He'd been wronged and wanted to get even. He wanted to find the truth.

He said, "Ask them myself."

Raven finally took the other chair. He met Montego on his level. The suggestion of a truce had turned into a full truce; they were allies, albeit temporarily. Montego was now an intelligence asset, and Raven needed to protect his asset.

"Okay," Raven said, "that's a deal. Let's work out how we'll do this."

"You've done this before?"

"It's not new to me, no."

"You're CIA?"

"Ex. I work on my own. That's why I told you my name."

Montego sat up and placed his elbows on the armrests of the chair, making a tent with his hands. He took a deep breath. "Aren't you supposed to alert your associate?"

Raven smiled and took out his phone. He sent a text to Tracy saying all was well. He put the phone back in his jacket. When he did, his hand brushed against the holstered Nighthawk Custom .45. He was glad he hadn't needed it—this time.

"All right, Mr. Raven. I'm ready."

31

LIA KENISOVA WRAPPED HER BODY IN A BIG TOWEL AND stepped out of the steamy bathroom. She was picking clothes out of a suitcase when somebody knocked on the door.

She and Darbo and Roger Justice were still in Oslo, trying to figure out their next move. Coming up with zero after hitting the warehouse wasn't the setback she wanted; however, recovering the rest of the nuclear parts was a win. But not the win they needed. Her head hurt from drinking too much after they returned, and the hotel bar staff had not appreciated her outbursts of Russian expletives as the night wore on. Roger and Darbo had been forced to drag her back to her room; Roger paid the tab.

"Who's there?" she called. She was only a few feet from the door. The hotel room wasn't large.

"Malikov."

She went to the peephole. Indeed, the FSB officer waited in the hallway, complete with long overcoat and hat. How long had he been in Oslo? Why hadn't he—but she dismissed the thought. The Russian spymaster was under no obligation to tell her anything.

"Hang on a minute, I'm not dressed."

"I'll wait."

Lia hurried to pull on her clothes, but didn't grab anything fancy. Jeans, T-shirt; quickly she tied back her hair and then answered the door. *Try not to look hungover*. Malikov removed his hat and entered.

"I didn't mean to disturb you, my dear," Malikov said.

"It's fine. I didn't know you were here." She locked the door and slid the chain in place.

"I thought I should stay in the background. Do you have any coffee?"

"I can make some." *I probably need a cup too*. She went to the coffee maker and busied herself with preparing a cup. The activity kept her occupied, which meant she didn't have to pretend to be sober for a minute or two.

"We recovered the rest of the bomb," Malikov said, "but nothing related to the location of the other triggers. There were no triggers in the warehouse we could find, and nothing to indicate where they might be located."

"But are we looking for a facility here, or somewhere else?"

"We don't know."

The coffee maker began percolating and filled the paper cup she placed under the spout. She didn't know where he was going with his statement, but waited for him to continue. The cup filled to the top, and she handed it to him.

"Thank you," he said. "Do you have any ideas?"

"We're at loose ends, too," she said, making another cup. While it filled, she stood in front of him and tried not to feel intimidated, but the overcoat over his stocky frame made him look like a brick wall.

"The Americans have the first two," Malikov continued. "We don't know if either of those were the original, or if the original is somewhere else, but we need it back."

"Are we at least talking to the Americans about this?" She folded her arms while Malikov considered his answer.

"We are, and it's diffused the situation. They're willing to help us keep a lid on it, as they say. But it's a matter of pride, you understand."

"Of course. Never doubted our reasons." She collected her cup and then couldn't decide how to hold it without looking silly.

"Ideas, my dear?"

"I can call Sam Raven."

"Why would he be of help?"

"He has contacts I don't. He might have heard something 'through the grapevine,' if you will."

"Feels like a desperate move."

"We wouldn't need a desperate move if we'd found what we needed at the warehouse," she said.

"Indeed. All right, do what you think is best. I'm on the plane back to Moscow tonight." He handed back the unfinished cup of coffee with a frown.

"No good?" she asked.

"Quite terrible. I should have brought some from home."

Lia glanced at her cup and wondered if she should bother.

THE COUNCIL for Economic Equality looked like a college campus. Large parking structure, open center courtyard, and a set of three buildings where all the action happened. They crossed the courtyard with Ernesto Montego in the lead. His face was stoic, his lips a flat light.

"I started this organization in good faith. Our first offices were in a strip mall, a dump with the walls falling in," he said. "To think my closest associates—"

Raven didn't interject. Montego didn't act like he was

faking his indignation. His anger was natural. He didn't have to put on a show to fool Raven. Tracy agreed, too.

"I've worked with these people for over a decade," Montego continued. They were walking toward the middle of the three buildings, which Montego earlier described as their administrative center. Raven and Tracy wouldn't be part of the meeting. They'd listen from a nearby office.

They had to listen to Montego and his associates and try to determine who was guilty, if any of them actually were. Raven was well aware he could be facing a rabbit trail to nowhere while the enemy continued moving toward their goal. According to Clark Wilson at the CIA, there'd been no sign of Cassiano La Bella anywhere after Tangier, which only confirmed Raven's earlier hypothesis. La Bella had big money behind him. He was a piece of a larger operation. And he'd vanished without a trace.

"We were united in a cause, a goal," Montego said. They were almost at the building. "This is a betrayal too close to home."

"Don't send them to the guillotine yet, Mr. Montego," Raven said. "Give them the benefit of the doubt until we know for sure."

"You're far more forgiving than I am, Mr. Raven."

"I've been in your spot many times."

"And the results?"

"Well—"

"I thought so."

Raven wanted to argue further, but the old man had a point.

As they walked, Raven noticed others milling about the courtyard, glancing their way, clearly recognizing Montego, but the council chief didn't see them. It was late in the day; everybody was off the clock. But Raven heard whispers in his mind. The ghosts of battles past were sounding an alarm.

The environment may have looked normal, but it wasn't. He glanced at Tracy. She met his eyes and nodded. She saw it too.

They were walking into a trap.

But what kind?

There was nothing to do but spring the trap and see.

The realization gave Raven hope. This visit wasn't a dead end after all.

MONTEGO SHOWED Raven and Tracy into an unused office with bare walls, a desk, and a telephone. He'd let them hear the meeting over the phone.

Montego left them and went down the hallway to his office, which was also on the spare side. He didn't go for big decorations, corner office with a window, none of that. He wanted to make sure the council spent its money where it belonged, on their programs. He wanted the money to help people. His desk was big and cluttered with no computer. Montego preferred not to use a computer at the office, but he had one at home.

He sat behind his desk and let out a breath. He opened a left-side drawer and removed a stack of paper, several items, and, finally, a black box in the back of the drawer. He raised the lid and looked at the Walther P-5 9mm pistol inside. The gun was scratched, with finish wear, but it still worked. He hadn't used a weapon since his youth but liked to keep it handy for the worst-case scenario. Like the one he faced now.

He checked the gun. Loaded. He stood and snapped back the slide to chamber a round. He put the gun in his right trouser pocket, but when he pulled his hand out, it was shaking. Yeah. He hadn't touched a gun in a long time; twenty-five years? At least. He kept the gun as a reminder of what he didn't want to go back to, but how else was he going to make the guilty party stay put until the police arrived? Montego took another breath and tried to mentally prepare himself for the confrontation ahead. He wasn't sure what he was going to say. He hoped he didn't need the gun. He hoped he was wrong. He hoped Raven needed to go and look somewhere else.

32

ERNESTO MONTEGO ENTERED THE CONFERENCE ROOM IN which he intended to have the meeting and stopped at the head of the table. A phone sat there, and he dialed the office in which Raven waited. Raven answered. Montego confirmed he and Tracy could hear him and asked Raven to press the mute button on his phone so nobody would hear them. He didn't care if any of his associates saw the red light indicating somebody was on the line. He didn't try to hide it.

He stood still and waited. The conference room was well-appointed; polished wooden table, black leather chairs, the carpet and walls also echoed a woodsy motif with their earth tones. The walls remained bare except for extra lights pointed at the ceiling.

A knock at the door. Montego called out, "Come in," and the door opened. The first of his associates entered.

Sasori Satoko was Japanese and wore a dark blazer and skirt over a white blouse with her hair tied back. She was his CFO, running the department in charge of the council's money. She approached the table and only said hello in her usual soft-spoken manner and sat down. She didn't ask what the meeting was about. Montego remained standing and watched her. She watched him. She was bright and efficient and dedicated to the council's cause. He didn't think she had a violent bone in her body. The only reason he suspected Sasori was because of her access to the money. She had no extremist activity in her background, no connections to the violent groups of Japan's past. The Liberation Faction of the Japan Socialist Youth League and the Japanese Red Army were both dead and gone, and no others had risen to take their places since. He didn't count the Aum Shinrikyo cult.

The next to enter was Axel Benitez, from Spain, who oversaw the management of the international teams the council sent around the world. If anybody was running a covert terrorist cell, it would be Benitez, only because he had access to a variety of individuals Montego never saw. He read their reports but couldn't say he'd recognize any of their names should they come across his desk. Could Benitez have somehow befriended Cassiano La Bella? The only opportunity the two would have had in Montego's presence was when Benitez gave a guest lecture to his class. It was a presentation of what the council was doing around the world. Benitez's lecture was a chance to promote the council's work, and the university didn't mind. After all, it was one of the primary reasons they'd hired Montego. They wanted the clout of being associated with a goodwill international charity. But Montego couldn't remember if the lecture was before or after Cassiano La Bella dropped out of his class.

Benitez was tall and trim with slicked-back hair and dark eyes. He was dressed in his usual business casual attire, with the collar of his shirt open a little. He sat opposite Sasori. Benitez had an uncle in prison for building bombs for Basque Separatists, but had never voiced support for political violence in the time Montego had known him.

Keeva Tully entered last, and her arrival was preceded by her loud voice. She was Irish, possessed a vibrant personality, and everybody knew when she was around because of her loudness. She ended a telephone conversation as she passed through the doorway and sat next to Sasori. She placed her phone on the table. A redhead, with freckles, she wore a brightly colored dress and sandals and crossed her pale legs as she settled in the chair.

She was another suspect. Keeva was from Northern Ireland, and didn't hide her connections to the former Irish Republican Army. Her father was active in Irish politics, but like Montego's own evolution, the Irish struggle against British occupation had gone from bombs to ballots. The current organization calling itself the Real IRA were more concerned about dealing drugs than fighting for "independence," and he'd never been impressed with the Irish fighters to begin with. Montego classified her as a "true believer." It was possible she wanted to set up her own terror cell.

"Thank you for joining me," Montego said.

Keeva spoke first.

"You look like somebody died, Ernesto." She smiled and tried to elicit a similar response from the others. Only Benitez acknowledged. Sasori remained stoic.

"I wish we were here to talk about good news," Montego said, addressing them all. "I'm afraid I have nothing to smile about this evening, until I get some questions answered."

Benitez said, "What's the problem?"

"More like 'who' is the problem, Axel."

Benitez frowned.

Montego put his hands behind his back and began to pace left-to-right, never leaving the head of the table.

"Some unfortunate news has come to my attention and I need the input of the three of you. One of my former students, Cassiano La Bella, is accused of becoming a terrorist." He stopped and looked at the three seated at the table. "You all know my background, and you all know how I've preached nonviolence ever since. Cassiano—he made me a promise, he promised not to ever follow in my footsteps, because there was a time when he very much wanted to. We had a long talk about it."

"What does this have to do with us?" Keeva asked.

"I need to know if any of you, or somebody else who is a part of our organization, encouraged Cassiano, gave him money, or put him in touch with anybody who encouraged his path to the dark side."

Benitez laughed.

"What's so funny, Axel?"

"Dark side? Are you kidding?"

"You'd know if you'd ever been there. I'm not quoting a movie. I'm serious. It simply happens to be the best analogy at this moment."

The three at the table remained silent.

"And you're not answering my question," Montego said. He met the eyes of all three, but they only blinked back at him. Perhaps it was time to raise the stakes. Turn up the heat. He needed an answer.

33

KEEVA TULLY SAID, "WHAT HAS THIS PERSON DONE? WHAT'S he accused of?"

Montego gave them a truncated edition of what Raven had told him.

"He's using a group of former students, they've apparently had some training, probably in the Middle East, and somebody provided weapons and money. I want to know who, and I want to know if it's any of you."

Silence.

"Are none of you even going to deny these accusations?"

"Why are you blaming us?" Benitez asked.

"Everybody involved with Cassiano so far has connections to my class and this organization. Some of them worked as interns here. It's enough for the authorities to initiate an inquiry, which means it's enough for me to begin my own investigation. I'd like to be able to get ahead of this and tell the authorities what's happening before suspicion falls on us, on me, and threatens everything we've accomplished around the world."

"I resent these accusations," said Sasori Satoko.

"I hate making them," Montego told her.

"Do you have any proof?" Benitez said.

"Do I need to look for any?" Montego countered.

"Nobody's going to be stupid enough to do what you're suggesting," said Keeva Tully.

"I wish I could believe that," Montego told her. "The fact is, of all of us, I'm the one with the most experience in violence. I know the thought process. I know what it's like to think you're too smart to get caught, and too smart for anybody to figure out what you're doing. The delusion works well until it's too late, and you're standing at the end of somebody else's gun."

The Walther in his pocket suddenly felt very heavy.

"All right," Montego said. No more pacing now. He faced the table. "I have no choice but to go to the authorities and invite them to start digging. I will not have this anvil hanging over my head any longer."

"You're weak, Ernesto."

Montego's eyes flared. Keeva Tully had spoken the words, and he felt heat rising within his chest.

"You call yourself a revolutionary, and maybe you were a good one," she continued, "but nothing will be achieved through talking. Talking never solved anything. Only action."

"Keeva—"

She rose, and Montego reacted on instinct. He reached into his pocket and pulled out the Walther P-5. He pointed the gun at her.

"Stay where you are, Keeva."

"Ernesto."

He snapped his eyes to Benitez, who'd produced his own pistol and leveled it at Montego's belly.

"She's right."

Montego started to swing the P-5 to the Spaniard, but Benitez fired first. The crack of the shot filled the room and

Sasori flinched and screamed. Keeva stood and watched. The bullet punched through Montego's belly and fell back against the wall. He tried to lift the Walter again, but a second shot from Benitez's handgun split his head open. Montego collapsed in a heap.

Sasori scrambled out of her chair so fast she knocked it over. Before she managed to run, Benitez shot her in the face. She landed face down with a splat. Keeva only gave the body a curious glance.

Benitez stood up. He said to Keeva, "Is everybody outside?"

"I was talking to them when I came in," she said, grabbing her cell phone once again. She held the phone to her ear and said, "It'll take us about twenty minutes to clear out our stuff."

"Get them all in here."

Keeva spoke into the phone. "It's time. Everybody come in."

Benitez went to the front of the table to look at Montego's body and bent down to pick up the man's Walther P-5. Rising, he spotted the phone. And the red light indicating somebody was on an inside line listening over the speaker.

"Who else is here?" he asked.

"What?"

"Somebody's been listening!"

The light didn't tell him which office the phone connected with, but it wouldn't be hard to find. He hung up the phone and waited for the extra troops to arrive. He'd send a few searching for Montego's spies while the rest gathered the evidence linking him and Keeva to Cassiano La Bella and, ultimately, Harrison Hunt.

RAVEN AND TRACY, in the other office, sat on the desk watching the phone. They were aware of who was who because of photographs Montego had shared, and they recognized gunshots when they heard them.

"What do we do?" Tracy said.

Raven said, "We need one of them alive."

"With all those people from outside coming in?"

"Let's not dwell on the odds."

Voices over the phone. Benitez and Tully:

"Who else is here?"

"What?"

"Somebody's been listening!"

The line clicked off.

Raven took out his .45 and went to the door. "They're on to us." Opening the door a crack, he peered into the hall beyond.

"I'm calling for backup," Tracy said. She pulled out her phone. She quickly called her contact at the embassy and gave an update. The Berlin CIA station was waiting for their SOS, but it would take time for them to get word to the local police. She and Raven would have to work fast unless they wanted to be arrested, or shot, with the rest of the terrorists.

"Good idea," Raven told her as he watched the line of men flow into the hall. He counted eight. Every other member of the group carried a submachine gun. If Benitez and the Irish woman needed to get material out of the building, it meant evidence was hidden within the offices. Taking one of the two masterminds alive wouldn't be as urgent as he thought.

He'd certainly not lose any sleep if he had to kill them all.

34

THEY HAD TO MOVE FAST. BENITEZ WOULDN'T NEED LONG TO issue orders. Staying in the office meant certain death. There was nowhere to run if they were cornered inside.

He eased the door open further to consider options. A fast run down the length of the hall ended at a bank of elevators and a stairwell. No cover available. And getting caught mid-run in the hall ended the same way—bad for them. A shorter distance away, across the hall and a jog to the right, was an open entryway leading to—what? Raven hadn't looked when they arrived, but it had to be better than the first option. With his gun in hand, he gestured to Tracy. She followed close behind, watching their back, her own pistol out and ready for action. They ran fast. The entryway led into a desk pool, mostly cubicles, a few darkened side rooms, and another wide entryway on the opposite side. Raven wanted a place to hide and wait for the enemy to come to him. Then he wanted one or even two of the submachine guns he'd seen. After he and Tracy acquired better weapons than pistols, they'd be evenly matched or, considering the caliber of fighters Cassiano La Bella brought with him to

Tangier, better. But Raven wasn't going to bet his life on the latter.

"This is lousy cover," Tracy said as they hustled behind a cubicle wall.

"Cover? It's not cover at all."

The cube wall concealed them only. The material wouldn't stop a bullet. Tracy broke away to find another such hiding place. They'd have a crossfire set up when the opposition came through.

They didn't have long to wait.

The four men with submachine guns strategized in the hallway, two breaking off to enter the desk pool. Raven watched through a narrow gap between two linked cube walls. The gunmen split up right away, one going left, the other following along the wall to the right. He was going to check the side rooms. The other was going to search the clusters of desks.

The desks and associated dividing walls were placed four to a cluster, with the other clusters spaced apart. Raven lost track of the second gunner as he moved deeper into the room, and wished he had some way of letting Tracy know a hostile was heading her way. He turned to watch the first, who used a small flashlight to peek into the side rooms while trying not to expose himself in a doorway. The process left his back facing Raven's direction. Raven moved to another cluster, staying low to avoid being seen over the top of a cube wall. The gunner followed the wall to the next side room, this time reaching around to flick a light switch and then enter in a crouch. Raven dashed from the cluster to the wall beside the room, staying quiet as the gunner searched. When the gunman exited, Raven clubbed him over the head with his Nighthawk .45. The gunner collapsed. Raven shot him in the head. The blast filled the room, and Tracy fired a string of shots, too. With the .45 holstered, Raven scooped up the dead gunner's submachine gun and spare ammo. He ran to Tracy, who was doing the same with the other gunner.

Shouting from the hallway signaled the other two were heading their way.

Raven and Tracy ran through the second entryway which led to a short hallway. On the other side, a cafeteria, the tables empty, the center serving counter clean, gleaming stainless steel. Before they cleared the hall, the remaining gunners opened fire behind them.

Raven tucked and somersaulted, launching to the left around a corner as he cleared the hall; Tracy's maneuver took her to the right, and they scrambled for cover. There were no cube walls this time. The lunch tables needed to be turned over. Raven knocked one over, then a second, before leaping across the center counter. The counter was a long U-shape. He didn't see where Tracy went.

The two gunners entered with one firing to cover the other. They shot at the overturned tables, only to find nobody hiding behind them. Raven rose and shot back, cutting one down before shifting to the other, who rolled out of the way. Raven's second burst chewed into a wall. When the last gunner brought up his weapon, Tracy took him out, firing off Raven's left. Her shots smacked into the gunner's shoulder and neck; he dropped. Tracy joined Raven behind the counter and they took time to reload.

"How many more left?" Tracy asked.

"Four, plus Benitez and Tully, weapons unknown."

"Benitez has a pistol."

"That's one for sure." Raven locked his fresh mag in place and racked the charging handle.

They left the counter and moved cautiously back the way they'd come, one covering the other as they advanced one at a time. Back in the desk pool, they used the clusters to conceal their movements while heading to the first entryway. There, Raven and Tracy stopped on either side, listening for the remaining opposition. Raven, hearing nothing, took a chance and peeked around the corner. Keeva Tully was in the hallway with a pistol and pulled the trigger. Raven jerked his head back and out of the way before the shot went off. Tracy fired back, exposing herself long enough to line up the Irish redhead in her sights. The lady killer didn't scream as she fell from the impact of Tracy's 9mm salvo.

Raven took the lead. Tracy followed him. The hallway made a 90-degree turn after the conference room. Raven wondered if the rest had gone that direction. The conference room was empty except for Montego's body; Raven resisted the urge to spare a thought for the ex-terrorist, though he had tried to do the right thing in the end.

AXEL BENITEZ DECIDED if he escaped alive, it would be a miracle. Right now, he wasn't sure of his odds.

One of his men guarded the door of his personal office, down the hall from the conference room. The man used Benitez's pistol. He'd given Montego's Walther P-5 to Keeva, and judging by the shots he'd heard, she hadn't survived. They had one man, one gun, and who knew how many coming for them?

Benitez and the rest of his crew stayed busy to not think about what was happening. They cleared boxes out of a closet and loaded the contents, papers and binders, into tote bags. The stack of totes grew; he no longer had enough people to carry them outside in one trip. But as they rushed to fill the totes, Benitez glanced at the office window. If he removed the screen, the window offered an avenue of escape. Or, at least, one of them had a chance to get away, and run off with the evidence while Benitez and the others went down with the ship.

He asked one of the men helping him to volunteer. One named Jacques did so, saying he'd prepared for such an escape by learning how to scale up and down a drainpipe. One such pipe was outside the window to the right, bolted to the exterior. Jacques said he could get outside, bring a car around, and they could drop the totes to him.

Benitez agreed and helped Jacques remove the screen from the window frame. Jacques stepped out, reached for the drainpipe, and started his fast trek down.

35

RAVEN DUCKED BACK AS PISTOL SHOTS FLASHED HIS WAY. ONE man at the end of the 90-degree branch, guarding an office door. Axel Benitez was still in the office, and Raven wanted him alive. The remaining crew members didn't matter. They wouldn't know anything useful.

"Let's rush the fucker," Tracy said.

Raven cut her off to get in front, moving low along the left wall while Tracy stayed to the right. They traded off firing 3-round bursts, one after another; the hail of lead chopped through the doorway and wall and cut down the lone defender. Raven reloaded on the run, Tracy letting go of the submachine gun to trade for her pistol. They swung into the spacious office to see Benitez tossing a black tote bag out the window, and his last two helpers ready to hand him another. Raven and Tracy set their smoking muzzles at the fresh targets.

Raven said, "Put that tote down, slowly, and put up your hands."

The man complied and dropped the tote and raised his hands.

With a grim set to his face, Axel Benitez lifted his hands to shoulder level, and Raven heard a car start outside. Whoever was on the receiving end of the totes was about to get away with some of the evidence. But Benitez's grin vanished when the shrill sounds of police sirens filled the campus below.

"Backup's here," Tracy said.

"Right on time," Raven replied. Approaching Benitez, he smacked the wanna-be terrorist with the butt of the submachine gun, and Benitez sprawled unconscious on the carpet. Raven looked out the window at the incoming cavalry. He told Tracy to call her connections at the embassy; they needed to make sure the cops didn't mistake *them* for the bad guys.

Getting mowed down by friendly fire would be a lousy way to fail the mission.

There was still a long way to go before they finished.

THE CLOCK on the wall matched Raven's watch; it was well after three a.m. Berlin time. He and Tracy looked exhausted enough to each resemble a burned dinner. But there was still work to do. They had to update Ops Officer Clark Wilson and Deputy Director of Operations Christopher Fisher at CIA headquarters. Benitez proved to be a goldmine indeed.

The basement of the US Embassy in Berlin housed a classified CIA work area, where Agency employees attached to the embassy could get their work done out of the prying eyes of standard-issue diplomats and staff. In a small office, sitting in front of a computer monitor, Raven and Tracy prepared to update the CIA men with what they'd learned over the past several tiring hours.

Wilson and Fisher weren't in a very good mood either. It

was early evening in Virginia, but both men had been on the phone to their Berlin counterparts, including those in the German intelligence services, almost as long as Raven and Tracy had interrogated Axel Benitez. The conversations had not all been friendly.

"We've called in so many favors with the Germans over this," Fisher said, "now we owe them a *lot*. This had better be worth it, Sam."

"We've been working on Benitez all night," Raven said, "but he cracked. This new terrorist group wasn't ready for prime time. You can teach them how to shoot a gun or set up a bomb, but withstanding interrogation is an art and science their trainers apparently didn't have time for. He gave us everything. The puppet master behind this scheme is somebody we all know, Harrison Hunt."

Fisher and Wilson took so long to reply, Raven thought the video connection had jammed. He didn't blame them for taking a moment. He hadn't believed the information either, until Benitez filled in the gaps.

"Are you joking?" Fisher said. "Why would Benitez name Hunt?"

Harrison Hunt was well known in the US, one of the billionaire celebrity class a great many of the population obsessed over until they learned how he voted. After becoming pals with a recent presidential candidate, Hunt quickly became a close adviser to the campaign, and then a policy adviser to the new administration when the country elected the candidate. Media controversy ended the relationship, though. When it appeared Hunt, unelected, had more to do with the president's decision-making process than anybody was comfortable with, media pressure and insistence from other close advisers pushed Hunt out of the administration and back to his ranch in Texas. Hunt remained a media darling despite the outcry and made the rounds of talk shows telling the world what the president should and should not do based on current situations. Hunt also continued to be a darling of the right wing and despised by the left.

"Because it's not a joke," Raven said. "In fact, it's probably the worst-case scenario. Hunt wants his own private nuclear arsenal."

"He wants a bomb?" Fisher asked.

"Two bombs."

"Why?"

"I'll get to it. He recruited Benitez, who recruited the rest of the gang, including Cassiano La Bella, and he used Evan Graham as a go-between to hide his involvement. He wants a pair of nukes to use as blackmail."

"Blackmail for what?" Clark Wilson said. "He has all the money—"

"Influence, Clark. He wants influence."

"As in," Fisher said, "he wants the government to pay attention to his policy ideas and wishes and desires or he'll shoot off a nuke?"

"Yeah," Raven said.

"If it was anybody but you, Raven, I think we'd all be laughing," Fisher said. "Either that, or you have the best poker face I've ever seen."

Tracy said, "He isn't lying, sir."

"We have video and a transcript to send," Raven said. "You'll get them shortly."

"Wait. How do Hunt and Graham connect?" Fisher asked.

"Hunt and Graham's father went to Harvard together," Raven said.

Fisher laughed nervously. "Um…Sam? We can't ask the FBI to pick up Hunt. Not on the word of a terrorist who might be throwing us a huge smokescreen. It's too crazy to be true."

"I think Benitez is telling the truth," Raven said.

"You believe a terrorist?"

"What's been Hunt's hobby the last fifteen years, Chris?"

The answer hit Fisher before Wilson, but Clark caught on when Fisher said, "Oh."

"Yeah. His own space program. Launching commercial payloads into orbit with unnamed rockets. He knows how rockets work and has people on the payroll who know more than him. If he wants to build a pair of nukes and only needed the trigger circuitry—"

"It's plausible."

"I'd like to point out, Chris," Raven said, "that I'm not held back by CIA rules or FBI red tape. Hunt is at his ranch outside San Antonio. I'm planning a flight right now."

"If anything happens to you, we don't know your name," Fisher said.

"Wouldn't have it any other way."

Fisher looked at Tracy. "Tracy? You get back to HQ. I want a full debrief."

"Okay," Tracy said.

"Sam? Get back with us if and when you discover what's going on, and I pray we aren't on a wild goose chase."

"We're sending the interrogation video and transcript. I'm sure you'll want to file it in the usual place."

"Where nobody can see it. Correct, Sam."

"Good luck, buddy," Wilson said.

Raven acknowledged and ended the video call. Tracy was looking at him, and it didn't take a rocket scientist to know what she was going to say. He cut to the chase.

"You're putting your career at risk if you ignore orders."

"If Hunt is the bad guy, if he's behind all of this, then he's the one responsible for the deaths of my team. I still owe them."

"And the rest?"

"I don't care."

"All right. Then let's get some sleep before we catch a plane to Texas."

"Yee haw," Tracy said, but without enthusiasm. They both needed a rest. Raven's phone ringing as they departed the basement office signaled the night was going deeper into overtime.

Raven frowned at the caller ID. "Lia? Is everything okay?"

"No, Sam, everything is a disaster, and we need help," the Russian woman said.

She told him the rest. Raven added more details she didn't know, since they'd been working the same case from different ends. He added that she, Darbo, and Roger should meet him in San Antonio. He wanted to show them some fancy horses. Lia pointed out she hadn't ridden a horse since her teen years and wondered if getting back in the saddle was like riding a bike. They both decided there was only one way to find out.

36

WATCHING THE HORSES DIDN'T PROVIDE THE USUAL tranquility Harrison Hunt craved after a long day.

There was too much on his mind.

Jack Moss and Cassiano La Bella were in the country; the quest was almost over. He'd received word from Moss earlier in the day. Their entry into the United States—through other than legal means—happened without a hitch. The arrangements had cost a lot, but they were worth the price.

The triggers were the last piece of the puzzle required to get his nukes online and ready for use.

He didn't plan to fire them. All he wanted was the threat they posed. He had ideas of how the United States in general, and the rest of the world in particular, should conduct themselves. The politicians of the world were too erratic. They couldn't make decisions without endless meetings, speeches, consensus, and the idiocy of the public. What the world needed was a single individual to make the final call, and Hunt had figured out how to fill the role.

He'd tried to exert his influence through the normal means, by having the ear of the president. But what had started as a good relationship leading to the end goal was ruined by interlopers within the administration working together to push him out. They used the media to do their dirty work.

Hunt then decided if politicians refused to listen to him one way, he'd make sure they listened another way.

It was one of the pluses of being the second richest man in the world.

He didn't plan to influence every decision or solve every conflict. The idea was to wait for the big issues, the major problems, the impasses. Then he'd whisper in this ear, that ear, and see to it the people involved knew which direction to go. If they refused, he had his private missiles to make sure they did as he wanted.

One might suggest all he needed was to pretend he had a pair of nukes at his disposal, but Hunt had learned a few things about politicians over the last two decades. They didn't respond to hollow threats. A threat needed teeth, so Hunt built himself a pair of sharp ones with which to chew his way through the gristle of resistance and the overcooked dedication to the status quo.

Building the rockets was easy. He had a company dedicated to unmanned space launches, and a list of public and government entities that used his company to pick up where NASA left off. Building the warheads, however, wasn't easy. The number of people he trusted for the project were few; such few hands caused no end to delays. He wasn't necessarily afraid of authorities crashing the party. His space company had several government contracts, but even more private contracts. The government knew he purchased rocket components on a regular basis, so he'd raised no suspicions with his purchases. It was the nuclear stuff he'd had to be careful about. More than careful. But they had accomplished the goal. Jack Moss and Cassiano La Bella were delivering those final pieces, and then Hunt could begin whispering.

Hunt wasn't only a billionaire businessman with a variety of companies and interests. His real passion in life was his horses. He watched them in the corral, as his trainers ran them in circles and back and forth through obstacles placed in the center. The animals kicked up a lot of dust, but he was too far away to have any of it in his face.

His ranch covered four hundred acres east of San Antonio, most of it overgrown forest; his house sat at the southwest end with an immaculate front yard, large pool in the back, and side buildings. The horse stables were approximately fifty yards from the house, with the corral adjacent. Big blue sky overhead. Peace and quiet. But Hunt felt troubled, the same sort of anxiety he always faced prior to the completion of a project. It didn't matter if it was his regular businesses—oil, construction, and tech, of which he owned several companies concerned with all three—or his current pursuit.

Cleaning up the loose ends, like Evan Graham, had been how he'd guaranteed no interference from the FBI or anybody else with a mind to put a stop to his plans.

He had no plans to eliminate Cassiano La Bella or his girlfriend. The young terrorist was useful and could remain so if he was smart enough to recognize a good opportunity. Someday he'd have Moss punch the kid's ticket, but for now it wasn't required.

The horses continued their maneuvers through the corral; two of his trainers steered their mounts back toward the stables.

Another cloud of dust caught his attention. A car traveled up the dirt road to the house. The guards at the gate along the interstate would have cleared them; it was Moss, making a report in person, as requested. Hunt retreated to the house to meet Moss at the front porch. The jowly man looked tired, but he shook Hunt's hand heartily after getting out of the car.

"Welcome home," Hunt said.

"I forgot how hot it is here. We hit San Antonio, and the heat smacked me like a runaway truck."

"But it's a clear day. And air conditioned inside. Let's get a drink."

They moved inside to Hunt's library. There was only one bookshelf. The rest of the shelves displayed Hunt's knick-knacks accumulated over the years. The furniture was made with high-quality leather. Hunt mixed the drinks, strong Manhattans. Moss said thank you and took a long sip. They sat on couches with a coffee table between them.

"This hits the spot," Moss said.

"What's the latest?"

"I got them squared away at a cottage thirty minutes from here. They're probably passed out in bed still."

"And the triggers?"

"They're secured at the place we arranged."

"Good. Bring Cassiano, his girlfriend, and the triggers to the underground site. I want them there before the sun goes down today."

"Okay."

"And then, keep them there. They don't leave. For any reason."

"Consider it done." Moss took another drink.

"Do you think Mr. La Bella will consent to further employment?"

"Hard to say," Moss said. "He's too much of a radical for me. He wants his payoff and a chance to build another cell in Europe."

"Hmmm." Hunt finally drank some of his Manhattan. He started to wonder if getting rid of La Bella should move to the top of the priority list. Hunt's plans did not include letting La Bella run wild in Europe. If he was caught, he'd talk. If he talked, he'd put Hunt in danger.

"Still want me to bring him to the underground site?" Moss asked. "Or do I get rid of him now?"

"You read my mind."

"Your decision?"

"Keep him contained for now. We'll decide the rest later."

"Fair enough."

Hunt nodded.

ANOTHER PAIR of eyes watched the ranch house from two hundred yards away. And the watcher took notes and pictures.

Zaven Darbinian, covered in a camouflage wrap to blend in with the terrain, watched Moss's arrival through binoculars. Trees and brush concealed him, birds chirped, critters shuffled through the dry brush and avoided him. The dirt was dry and hot from the beating of the sun.

A camera recorded the visitor's arrival as well, and Darbo made a mental note of Moss's appearance to relay to Sam Raven and the others at their safehouse.

He didn't know who Moss was or if he was important, but Raven wanted to know who showed up, how long they stayed, and he wanted it all on video. Once they identified the fellow, maybe they'd know a little more about Hunt's friends. But if the visitor was simply another tycoon or a poker buddy, they were wasting the day.

But Darbo had a feeling the visitor was important.

They'd find out soon enough.

Lia had secured the safehouse upon their arrival in Texas. They were staying in a small town in Medina County, using a pair of rental cottages with most of the necessary amenities.

Reaching the ranch only took a thirty-minute drive along a two-lane highway through beautiful country. It was easy to get caught up looking at the greenery and tall mountains and almost lose sight of what they were there for.

Almost.

Darbo stayed until Moss left, and Hunt went back to watching the horses. Darbo noticed Hunt was smiling, where he hadn't been smiling before.

Darbo pulled a handheld radio from the front pocket of his camouflage blouse. "Heads up. Visitor leaving."

"I got a lock on him," replied Roger Justice. The American mercenary's position was further away, close to the interstate road leading past the ranch. "The drone is ready to track."

Darbo acknowledged. He wanted to wait a little longer to see if anybody else showed up before heading back to the others.

CASSIANO LA BELLA HAD NEVER SEEN SUCH A SMALL TOWN AS Medina, Texas. One main street, no stoplights, a post office, three bars—he supposed it was typical to have that many— and one church. The rental cottage Moss found for them was off the road and behind a cluster of trees, so they at least had a little privacy. Moss said they had no enemies to worry about. They were in Hunt country, and even the small towns within spitting distance of the big ranch somehow did business with him. They looked out for their main source of income.

Enemies coming to the door weren't top of mind for Cassiano as he sat on the porch chair and stared into the distance. There were mountains out there, and they battled with the sky for supremacy. His thoughts were on the other side of the world, in Berlin, because news of what took place at the offices of the Council for Economic Equality had reached him. The shootings were a major part of the European news for the day. He had consumed the video footage, live reports from the scene, and written accounts.

All he knew for sure was his friends and mentors were gone. Dead.

Montego. Axel. Keeva. Gone. The official story didn't ring true, not one piece. The Germans wanted people to believe a right-wing motivated mass shooting had taken place, suspects still at large; Cassiano knew the truth. Sam Raven had been there. Politics had nothing to do with the killings.

He was on his own, like an orphan, though he dared not say so out loud knowing his real parents were still alive. But his revolutionary parents were gone, taken by enemy bullets. Once they handed the trigger circuits over to Harrison Hunt, his obligations fulfilled, he wanted to take Simona and go look for Sam Raven full time. The hell with anything else until Sam Raven was dead at his feet.

If he had to shoot his way out of Texas to get what he wanted, so be it.

Nothing else mattered but revenge.

Simona stepped out onto the porch. The door squeaked a little. "Are you all right?"

He considered it a stupid question but wasn't about to tell her. "A lot has happened, Simona. A lot of stuff in the last few weeks. It's taking a toll."

"I know." She left the doorway to sit next to him.

"I don't know how much more of this I can take."

"This is what you wanted," she said. "But it's also what Montego told you would happen, and why he made you promise not to follow in his footsteps. But here we are."

"He was right about a lot of things. Once we're done here, we're going after the American."

"He'll come to us," Simona said.

"You think Axel or Keeva talked?"

"Somebody did. Even Moss thinks so."

He turned to her, alarmed. "Did you tell him?"

"That's why I came out here. He called. He's done with

Hunt and coming back. We need to get ready to go because we're leaving as soon as he gets here."

"To do what?"

"He didn't say, but we need to be ready."

"What is he hiding?"

"You'll have to ask him, Cass."

"You know I will."

ROGER JUSTICE'S custom-made drone contained a small camera in the nose and the ability to fly on autopilot while tracking a moving target. The tracking system worked much like a laser-guided bomb, where an infrared dot placed on a moving target created a "leash" for the drone, and the craft followed the marked vehicle while at the same time flying high enough to avoid obstacles.

Roger reported the drone was flying back to Medina; he projected Moss was staying either at the same row of cottages as Raven's team, or he was staying at another. He and Darbo drove back to Medina, eventually catching up with Moss's car. They entered the town limit at the same time. Moss turned into a row of rental cottages on the right side of the road, and his car vanished behind a tree line. Roger and Darbo continued up the street and turned into a row of cottages on the left side of the road. If the stroke of coincidence had gone the other way, they might have been next door.

Roger recalled the drone, making sure it stayed high enough to avoid trees and telephone lines and not be obvious to anybody on the ground.

Roger and Darbo found Raven in the first of their two cottages with Tracy and Lia. Each cottage sported old-world décor with hardwood flooring. The men stayed in one, the women the other. Raven wanted everybody prepared for action at a moment's notice, so individual packs containing weapons and ammunition sat near the door.

Roger brought his drone inside and set it near the kitchen while Darbo carried his gear to the kitchen table. Darbo began verbally filling in Raven and the women about what he witnessed. While he spoke, Roger found a seat at the front window to watch Moss's cottage. It was tough to see through the cluster of trees, but saw enough. If Moss moved, he'd alert the others.

Darbo hurried to set up his laptop.

Raven asked, "Who showed up?"

Darbo glanced at Raven, who stood over his shoulder while he booted up the computer. "Somebody we don't know yet," the Armenian mercenary replied. He tried not to sound sarcastic.

"Sorry," Raven said. "Let's hope the emphasis is on *yet*."

"If a record of him exists, we'll identify him."

The computer finished booting and Darbo selected the video file. There was plenty to watch if anybody wanted to see the horses practice, but Darbo knew nobody did, so he jumped to the middle of the video file where Jack Moss arrived. He caught a decent shot of Moss's face as he stole a glance back upon entering the house with Hunt. Darbo froze the video there and captured Moss's face with the screen snipping tool. He enlarged the photo and fed the file into a software program that would compare Moss's face to those in the FBI database, as well as Interpol's, to see if the man had a criminal record. If he did, they'd know his name.

The FBI database spit back a result right away. Everybody except Roger gathered behind Darbo to see.

"This is a good one," Darbo began. "John Jacob Mosselli, currently going by the name Jack Moss. Formerly with an organized crime syndicate in New Jersey. Served fifteen years for murder."

"Who did he kill?" Tracy asked.

"His father."

"Related to a syndicate problem?" Raven asked.

"Personal conflict, it says here. Dad wasn't a gangster."

Roger yelled, "They're moving!"

Raven ran to the window to see. Sure enough, Moss's car was backing out. He turned back to the others. "Grab weapons and ammo and split into both cars!"

The team scrambled for their gear.

38

WHEN MOSS ENTERED THE COTTAGE, HE FOUND CASSIANO and Simona sitting at the kitchen table. Cassiano appeared upset.

"What's the problem?" Moss asked.

"Don't worry about it," Cassiano told him.

"Set it aside for later. We have work to do."

"I said, *don't worry about it*. What did Hunt tell you?"

Moss decided not to argue about the kid's state of mind any further. He was depressed about events in Berlin, and Moss understood—to a point.

Moss said, "Get your stuff. We're leaving."

"Are we coming back?"

"Nope. Don't forget anything."

"What did Hunt say?"

"We're going to him." A red flush crept up Moss's neck, but he settled down. Why couldn't the kid simply follow orders? "Now get moving."

None of them had unpacked, so all they had to do was gather suitcases and Cassiano his backpack, which contained a few personal items for both him and Simona. It took seconds to grab the luggage, but Moss took a minute to make sure they hadn't left any loose items behind, and his search quickly satisfied him they had not.

"Where are we going?" Cassiano asked.

"It's a secret," Moss told him. He went out, leaving the front door open.

Cassiano and Simona exchanged glances, but Cassiano shook his head. He didn't think they had anything to worry about.

"Move it!" Moss called from the car.

Cassiano and Simona moved it.

FOLLOWING MOSS'S car created a new set of problems.

A two-lane road led out of Medina, with open country and forest on either side, a beautiful sight, but the lack of traffic meant Raven and the others had no real traffic to cover their work. Raven and Darbo and Tracy drove one car, while Lia and Roger drove the other. Connected by radio, Raven issued instructions as Darbo, driving, let Moss have some distance. The open road allowed them to see Moss's car despite the gap.

"We'll turn off ahead," Raven said into the radio, "and you two stick with Moss. We'll catch up again, then you disappear for a bit. He's going to make us fast otherwise."

"He'll know we're following anyway," Lia said.

"This way we buy some time."

"You hope," the Russian woman said.

"Maybe if you hope too, we can get it done."

Lia continued, "It won't be long before we have more traffic. And he doesn't have anywhere to go, same as us."

"You know the drill, Lia. I have a feeling they're not coming back this way."

Raven set the radio on his lap and cursed. Following Moss could go sideways. If they lost him, he wasn't sure where to go next. The only option would be a raid on Hunt's mansion, and he didn't want to go to such an extreme. Hunt had innocent employees around. Raven considered the armed security staff non-combatants; they hadn't signed up to repel a commando force. They probably had no idea what Hunt was doing. He wasn't about to go blasting at guys trying to make a living.

"We can't lose him," Raven said.

Darbo replied, "We won't."

But Raven knew it wasn't going to be so easy.

CASSIANO AND SIMONA sat in the back seat while Moss drove. Simona clutched his left hand; Cassiano watched the passing scenery. Lots of tall green grass. Lots of thick trees, some of which had split and grown into a monstrous mash of twisting branches. If Moss wanted them dead, several proper opportunities had passed. No. Moss wasn't taking them to the middle of nowhere for a bullet in the back of the head. First, they had to collect the trigger circuits. Then, Cassiano figured, it was time to either meet Harrison Hunt as Moss stated or visit the site where the missiles awaited their triggers. In other words, the last leg of the mission, the end of the road, the chance to prove he was worthy. Worthy of his pay, worthy of being a major contender for future missions, with or without a sponsor's support.

All the work, and especially all the sacrifices, were about to pay off. The victory was for all of his friends who fell striving for the goal.

He brought Simona's hand to his lips and kissed her fingers. His grin was infectious; she smiled, too. He wondered if she felt the same way he did. Now certainly wasn't the time to celebrate out loud, but soon...

"WE HAVE A TAIL," Jack Moss announced.

Cassiano started to turn—

"Don't look!"

Cassiano sat forward and let go of Simona's hand.

A tail? Was it Raven?

Was the American coming to him like Simona said?

"If it's Raven, we need to make a stand," Cassiano said.

"If it's Raven," Moss countered, "he's not alone. Wait. The car just made a left. We might be okay."

"*Might be okay* is not a good strategy, Jack."

They traveled Texas Highway 16 along the Medina River, on their way to Bandera, a town with less than 1000 people where Moss had stored the trigger circuits. From there, they'd head toward San Antonio with a jog east. The problem? They were traveling through the boondocks. But if Sam Raven had caught up, there were also plenty of spots along the way to make the stand Cassiano advocated.

But Moss had another idea...

HARRISON HUNT MADE A SIMPLE DEMAND: "Tell me what's happening?"

Moss drove with one hand and held his cell to his ear with the other. He didn't want Cassiano to hear Hunt's end of the conversation. The kid would argue.

Moss explained: "We have two cars doing a trade-off surveillance drill."

"Raven?"

"Probably."

"Do you have the triggers?"

"We picked them up in Bandera. These two cars have been with us one way or another since we left Medina, which means they've been on to us for a bit. If they haven't made a move, they're more interested in where we're going than recovering the triggers. How about you arrange a reception for them?"

"I don't want to expose the tunnels."

"Harrison, we need the numbers. I got three against five here. If they engage, forget your triggers."

"All right. Proceed. Let them follow, and I'll set up the ambush."

"See if they can warn me before they open fire."

"Do not participate, and do not let La Bella out of the vehicle. Your priority is getting the triggers to me."

"Count on it."

"If you fail…"

"We won't."

THE ROAD REMAINED one lane each direction, twisting and turning through hills, straightening through open fields; they passed several ranches, announced by arched gates, big signs, and a display of the ranch's brand symbol.

Raven told Darbo to give Moss at least a quarter mile lead, but they had the same problem as when they'd left the Medina town limit. They were the only two other cars on the road. A few passed in the opposite direction, but one thing was clear. Moss had to know they were hostile by now. But for some reason, he was leading them on.

Leading them into…

Raven grabbed the radio.

"Heads up! We're heading into an ambush!"

Tracy, in the back seat, opened her pack to extract her submachine gun. She already had her Glock pistol on her right hip. Raven asked for his pack, and she hefted it over the front seat. He took it from her.

"They're taking a big risk doing this," she said.

"Which means we'll be outnumbered twenty to one," Raven said. He removed his weapon from the pack. As usual, the Nighthawk Custom .45 autoloader rode in a harness under his left arm.

Darbo said, "Those poor bastards don't stand a chance."

Raven forced a laugh he didn't feel.

And then the ambush started.

39

THE RIFLE GRENADE ZEROED ON THE FRONT OF RAVEN'S CAR, but at the last second fell short.

The explosive landed on the asphalt, the explosion tearing a hole in the pavement. The shock of the blast flung Raven's car off the road, the vehicle tipping to the right as it crashed through a barbed wire fence and onto the grassy field beyond. The car continued tipping onto its roof and then struck a rise which flipped it back onto its wheels. The car landed with a jolt and remained still, window glass shattered, the passenger side cratered; nobody inside moved.

In the second car, Roger slammed the brakes as another rifle grenade sailed at him and Lia. The grenade overshot and detonated in the field behind them. Roger watched with wide eyes as armed men emerged from holes in the ground on the left side of the road, running to the barbed wire blocking the field from the pavement. A few opened fire and bullet strikes rocked the car. Lia shouted at him. Roger broke from his stare and went into action. He followed Lia out the passenger side door, both grabbing their combat packs from the back seat.

Lia had her HK416 out before Roger. She braced around the front bumper and triggered short bursts at the incoming threats. The car cut off part of her view; she couldn't count the total number, but there were plenty to keep them occupied. Roger joined the fight, positioned at the bumper, firing steadily, his HK416 bucking against his shoulder.

Roger took down two of the gunmen. He watched their bodies tumble into the grass. The others rolled for concealment in the tall grass and returned fire. Roger sprayed a burst at random, probing for a target; his burst didn't connect, so he shifted his aim and fired again. A head popped up as a gunner made a dash for the fence. Roger pulled the trigger and took the man down. As the gunman hit the ground, a grenade rolled from his hand and tumbled for the fence. It detonated short but tore up a chunk of dirt a few feet away.

Roger ducked back to reload. As he slapped the fresh magazine home, he stole a glance back at Raven's car. It remained on its wheels. It remained still.

"Cover me!" Lia shouted. She dropped back to reload, and Roger opened fire again. They needed this fight done so they could check on Raven and the others. If it wasn't already too late...

RAVEN'S WORLD became a kaleidoscope of chaos as the car rolled; airbags exploded in front and on each side, pulling a hot curtain over the rotating images around him. The smack of the airbag on the right side of his head stung; his face slammed into the bag deployed from the dash. Tracy screamed in the back, but then her screaming stopped, cut off sharply, as if a switch flipped and turned her off. Darbo uttered nothing during the side-over-side tumble, and when the car finally jolted to a landing on all four wheels and Darbo slumped against his seat belt, Raven feared the worst.

"Tracy!"

"Still here!"

Raven groaned and tried to move, but his body felt like Jell-O and his eyes wouldn't focus.

Gunfire cracked.

"We gotta get out, Raven!"

Raven shut his eyes, opened them, and began pushing away the bulk of the deflated airbags around him.

"Raven!"

"I'm trying!"

Everything hurt as he moved, but he finally pushed open the passenger door and let the outside air into the car. The gunfire was louder now, but none of the shots were coming their way. Darbo groaned and lifted his head, Raven looking back at his friend as he rolled out onto the grass. The blades of grass poked at him; he sat up, rose, and leaned against the smashed fender. He looked at the road and the fight taking place only twenty yards away.

Enemy gunners in green camo needed to get through the barbed wire to reach Roger and Lia, but faced a heavy dose of fire. Darbo, still behind the wheel of Raven's car, shouted Raven's name and shoved his HK416 across the passenger seat. Raven took the weapon and his pack and began the slow trudge forward, the high grass whipping at him. He slipped through the barbed wire, tearing part of his jacket, rolling into the drainage ditch, he braced his weapon on the edge of the road.

His first salvo startled Lia, who swung her head back to look at him. He pointed forward, and she turned back to engage the oncoming fighters, or what remained of them. Raven saw a lot of bodies in the grass, but had no way to tell which ones were corpses and which were fighters under cover.

Raven unzipped a pocket on his pack and withdrew one of the four grenades inside. Pulling the pin, he tossed it overhead, grabbed the HK, and triggered careful shots as the grenade sailed across the road. The blast sent a load of shrapnel into some of those under cover bodies and resulted in screams and flailing arms and legs before the bodies lay still once again.

Movement on his left. Raven looked. Tracy, with her submachine gun, joined the right on Roger's left flank.

"Hold your fire!" Lia shouted.

Raven stopped, keeping his head low, and scanned his view of the battleground. Roger and Tracy held back on their shooting as well, and as the echo faded, the wind took over. The gunmen were dead. Raven reloaded and rose on shaky legs. He removed gear from his back, his battle harness, extra ammo, and strapped everything into place.

"Where do you think you're going?" Lia asked.

"Where they came from," Raven said with a dismissive gesture at the field on the other side of the road.

"We're tunnel rats now?"

"Somebody needs to stay with Darbo," Raven said. "He's hurt. I'm going in there even if I have to go alone."

"Your head is scrambled," Lia said.

"No, it's fine. Gives me superpowers." Raven started to lose his balance but rested a hand on the hood of the car to steady himself. Lia raised an eyebrow. Raven shook his head. "There's nothing else we can do, Lia."

Roger and Tracy joined them.

"We going in?" Roger asked.

"I need a volunteer to stay with Darbo," Raven repeated. He straightened and didn't feel dizzy. His vision was still wonky, though.

"I'll stay," Lia said. "I got him into this mess."

"All right," Raven said. "Roger, Tracy, follow me."

Raven ducked under the barbed wire on the opposite side, realizing how close the opposition had come to breaking through and finishing Lia and Roger. The three ran through the grass, moving around bodies, until they came to an open trapdoor in the middle of the field. The door was made of wood, well concealed with fake grass attached to the top, hinged within a square wooden frame. A set of steps led into a dark tunnel below ground; Raven attached a flashlight to his HK rifle, and Tracy and Roger followed.

Raven took the first step down.

THE AIR SMELLED musty the farther they descended, the narrow tunnel braced with a wooden frame along either side, which held up a long wooden plank creating a ceiling. Steel clamps in the frame added structural strength. Raven decided whoever built this tunnel meant it to last a while. It reminded him of old mineshafts he'd toured as a young man; but this tunnel would take them only to the next stage of the fight. And hopefully the final confrontation with Cassiano La Bella and Harrison Hunt.

The bright flashlights highlighted the way, but the illumination only extended so far. A constant cloud of dust surrounded them. Raven, Tracy, and Roger used one hand to cover their faces, but their eyes still stung. Darkness remained ahead; they were walking into a void. Raven's breathing came faster, his pulse quickening; Tracy and Roger were also breathing harder. Part of it was from being underground. Part of it was from not knowing what lay ahead but knowing they had to press on regardless.

A loud squawk filled the tunnel. Raven stopped. Tracy

and Roger halted, and Roger raised his flashlight beam to look at the ceiling. A speaker.

"I'm glad I get to finally meet you, Mr. Raven and companions."

Raven wondered if he should reply, but decided against doing so.

"Keep moving forward. I have people waiting for you."

"I suppose it wouldn't do any good to turn around," Raven muttered, glancing at Tracy and Roger.

"No, Mr. Raven, it wouldn't. And, yes, I can hear you."

"Your voice sounds different on the TV, Mr. Hunt," Raven called out.

"Wait till you see me face-to-face. Keep moving, please."

Raven lowered his weapon. There was no reason to prepare for a fight. Where they were going, they'd be outgunned. Hunt would make a long speech about how big of a badass he was, and then the firing squad. All Raven wanted was a showdown with Cassiano La Bella. A cage match. A chance to break the little terrorist's neck before the end came for him, too.

He hoped Darbo and Lia were okay.

"Let's go," he said, and took the lead once again.

40

"WE'RE SURRENDERING?" TRACY WHISPERED AS SHE CAUGHT Raven's stride.

"I didn't say we were surrendering, Tracy."

"So we're going to—"

"Wing it this time, yeah."

Roger said nothing. Raven looked back at him. "No comment?"

"We've pulled it off before, boss," the American mercenary said.

They finally came to a steel door. It was open a crack. Raven reached for the handle and pulled. Bright light entered the tunnel; he squinted, waiting for his eyes to adjust. Stepping forward onto a solid floor, he noted the four gunmen standing in front of him with their gun muzzles leveled at his belly. They held rough-looking Uzi submachine guns. An older man stood off to the side, and he smiled at Raven.

"Your hair doesn't look as gray on television, Mr. Hunt," Raven said.

"I have an expert makeup girl," Hunt said.

The room was all steel, like the airlock of a submarine. Bright lights overhead, a cool breeze from vents along the ceiling. Raven, Tracy, and Roger handed their weapons to one of the gunmen who stepped forward, slinging his own as he collected theirs. The other gunmen moved in and stripped the trio of their combat rigs and handguns. Raven was shoved against a wall, but put his hands out before impact. Tracy and Roger were shoved next to him.

"You may turn around," Hunt said.

Raven was the first to do so. He made eye contact with Hunt and said, "What now?"

"Now you get to see what all the fuss is about. You get to see what all my work has been leading to, and what will be impossible to stop once I make it known, for the first time in history, that an *individual* is a nuclear power. Fascinating idea, isn't it?"

"Sure," Raven said. "It's what the Second Amendment is all about."

Hunt laughed. "Well, the Founders certainly didn't only have *muskets* in mind when they wrote it, did they?"

Hunt led the way out of the room, his gunmen trailing behind Raven, Tracy, and Roger, as they traveled along a corridor with a metal floor and rock walls. Activity echoed from ahead, and they rounded a corner and stopped in the middle of a large work area, circular in shape, the center further sank into the ground while a raised platform served as a control center and observation station. A large conveyor belt extended from the center of the circle into another tunnel. Lined up in front of the conveyor belts were two long missiles.

Men in lab coats fussed around the pair of stainless steel missile tubes. The nose cones were separate from the rest of the missile bodies, and exposed circuitry extended from the open ends of both body and cone. The white-coated engineers weren't carrying weapons, and were too focused to notice the audience Harrison Hunt had brought to them.

Raven glanced around. Walkways above, ringing the open space. Armed men walked back and forth at a slow pace. He mentally noted the gunmen behind them. They were outgunned for sure, but there were enough nooks and crannies within which to hide that they actually had a fighting chance if they played their cards correctly.

"Where are we?" Raven said.

"This is the assembly area. As you can see, the tunnel continues around to the left."

Raven looked along the extension. "What's down there?"

"The launch area," Hunt said.

"Why two missiles? Is one for demonstration? You going to blow up New York City?"

"No. When the trigger circuits are installed, the missiles will be placed on the conveyor belts you see and transported into the launch area. From there, they'll rest on platforms till they're ready."

"You actually rigged—"

"The earth will open, and my missiles will fly freely, Mr. Raven. It's not unlike the military silos in the Midwest."

"Why do you have two missiles?"

Hunt shrugged. "Because I can. Because if I need to use one, the world will know I still have another."

"But *why* do you need missiles?"

"Our leaders are feckless wonders," Hunt said. "Now and then they're going to need somebody to make a final decision, and if they try to push back—well, you don't say no to somebody who has a set of nuclear bombs in his backyard. And the will to use them."

"Against whom?"

"Does it matter?" Hunt said. "All they need to know is that I'll pull the trigger if they don't do what I say."

"So, this is your way of throwing a tantrum. You're just a big baby? Don't look at me like you're confused, Hunt. You got kicked out of the White House, so you've taken these steps to hold on to whatever power you think you had. Am I close?"

"Go on."

"But who did you let into your house to make this happen? Do you have any idea who Cassiano La Bella really is? Now that he's done helping you, you can bet he's plotting how to steal these rockets for himself."

Hunt laughed. "Never happen."

"He's a time bomb. He'll blow up in your face before you realize what's happening."

"Speaking of which—"

Hunt turned his attention to the extended side of the tunnel, and Raven spotted shadows crawling along the steel floor. Cassiano La Bella, his girlfriend Simona, and Jack Moss walked into view. When Cassiano locked eyes with Raven, he didn't need an introduction. They both knew each other. Tracy's eyes locked onto the young terrorist as well.

"Mr. Raven, I'm afraid Mr. La Bella hasn't stopped talking about you since he arrived," Hunt said. "He was very upset about the ambush."

"Not so upset about the results," Cassiano said. He and Raven faced each other like a pair of lions about to fight over a meaty carcass.

"I think I have an idea," Hunt said. He checked his watch. "The trigger circuits will be installed within the hour. After we clear the missiles out, we'll have enough room for a private match between the two of you. If you win, Cassiano, life goes on. But, Raven, if you win, it only means one thing."

"What?" Raven asked.

"You'll be the next to die."

THE ENGINEERS INSTALLED the trigger circuits on time and attached the nose cones to the missile bodies. Power drills *whirred* and made an echoing racket as the engineers screwed the nose cones into place. Raven shook his head, watching with interest despite the action taking place in front of him. What had once been sophisticated and impossible to consider for all but the best and brightest could now be built by any nuclear expert who didn't care what the weapon was intended for. The chance to build one for any reason, funds unlimited, was enough to motivate the white-coated crew to do the bidding of Harrison Hunt. And not a whistleblower among them.

The missiles rested on large rolling chassis units. The chassis were motorized, so when the engineers guided the now fully functional nuclear missiles to the conveyor belt, they didn't have to push. The missiles, lined up with the belt, began the slow migration from the work facility to whatever lay beyond. Raven, Tracy and Roger watched the missiles disappear into yet another tunnel, this one leading to the launch pads. Raven almost sensed defeat; but they weren't out of action yet.

Tracy, standing beside Raven, whispered, "This is insane."

"I don't believe it myself," he told her.

"But it's happening."

"Yup."

Harrison Hunt broke into their conversation. "And now, as promised, we have the chance for Mr. Raven and Mr. La Bella to settle their differences in one-on-one combat."

"In the center of the circle?" Raven asked.

"Floor is smooth. You have a rail surrounding it, much like a boxing ring. What's not to like?"

"Hand-to-hand or choice of weapons?" Raven said.

"You're more sporting than I realized, Mr. Raven."

"One condition."

Hunt raised an eyebrow.

"If I lose, my people go free."

Hunt shook his head. "Can't do it, Mr. Raven. They've seen everything. They cannot leave here alive."

Raven nodded. "I expected nothing less." He turned to Tracy and Roger, who only nodded back. Everybody was on their own once the fight started.

Cassiano La Bella shouted, "Knives! We'll fight with knives." He took an aggressive step forward, but Simona put a hand on his arm. He stepped back.

"That's fair," Raven agreed.

Hunt went to two of his guards and collected the knives from their belts. He gestured for both Raven and Cassiano to go down the short walkway to the sunken center of the chamber. Raven let the young terrorist go first. When they reached the wide circle, they turned back. Hunt tossed them their knives. They landed on either side of the "ring," and both scrambled to grab them.

Cassiano grabbed his first. He ripped the blade from its leather sheath and rushed at Raven.

RAVEN ONLY HAD a moment to examine his blade before Cassiano La Bella made his rush. The weapon was a standard Ka-Bar, with a leather wrapped handle; he'd used one before. The edge of the blade glinted in the bright overhead light. Cassiano's rush wasn't good form; he wanted to overwhelm Raven with speed and fury. He only cared about the chance to slice Raven's throat and watch him bleed out all over Harrison Hunt's shiny floor.

But the kid was making yet another mistake.

Raven dodged backward as Cassiano's first thrust swept within inches of his face. While Cassiano had his blade toward the ground, caught in the open with no way to defend his torso, Raven struck with a backhand blow. He connected solidly with Cassiano's face, sending the young terrorist off course with an unexpected spin.

Raven started forward to get an arm around Cassiano's neck and end the fight with a slash across his throat, but the younger man recovered fast. He spun back toward Raven, executing a perfect roundhouse kick and Raven felt the world spinning once again. He landed hard on the steel floor, breath rushing out of his lungs, and only his combat senses screaming for him to move kept him from further injury.

He rolled as Cassiano tried to stomp on his back. Raven shifted so his feet faced Cassiano's direction, delivering a kick to the younger man's left knee. Cassiano screamed and shifted, staying on his feet as he bounced back and shuffled like a boxer. Raven rolled to his feet, his knife clenched in a tight fist, the blade angled down, awaiting Cassiano's next move.

Cassiano shifted on his feet, eyes locked on Raven; if the kid was trying to scare him, it wasn't working. Raven didn't have a moment to get nervous. He had to make sure he struck at the correct Cassiano when the time came, because he was seeing double.

This probably wasn't a good idea...

Raven stepped backward, conscious now of eyes on him. Not only his people and Hunt and Hunt's four guards, but some of the white-coated engineers had made their way back. Some watched from one of the upper walkways, leaning over the safety rail for a better view.

Can't let down our audience...

"Come on, kid," Raven called, his back to the rail around the center circle. There was no safety there, with Cassiano's girlfriend so close to guns, but it helped him keep the kid in front of him. "Let's finish this."

"Get closer." Cassiano made a few fancy swipes with his knife, but Raven didn't blink. His vision straightened out a little.

"You should have heard your buddy Axel squeal to the Berlin police."

"You're lying! He never would have talked."

Raven laughed. And it was the mocking laugh Cassiano reacted to. He lunged at Raven with a twisted snarl on his face.

Raven moved in aggressively as well, meeting Cassiano halfway and the two men furiously slashed and stabbed; ducked and dodged; the knife blades clashed, but no razor edge found flesh; no sharp point split skin to cut into organs. Raven backed off, same as Cassiano, and had to admit the kid was good. But this dance back and forth had to end sometime.

The gladiators circled each other again. Raven tried a new approach.

"Montego was disappointed in you, Cassino. He almost cried. You were his favorite. He said of all his students, you were the one who'd be great, but only if you ditched your dreams of being a mass murderer."

Cassiano stepped forward and jumped back, each time putting Raven on guard; he breathed hard, his jaw clenched tightly, and Raven wondered if his words were breaking through.

And then Cassiano lost what little self-control he had.

"No!" He charged, holding the knife low, going for an upthrust by the time he reached Raven.

Raven blocked Cassiano's wrist with his left hand, and thrust his blade forward and back once, twice, a third time. Color drained from Cassiano's face as the shock hit him; the pain followed, and then he staggered back unsteadily while trying to scream through an open mouth. He failed to get any noise out. Raven moved in for the kill. Grabbing Cassiano's right shoulder, he spun the younger man around and pulled him close, then slashed the blade across the terrorist's neck. He stepped back and let Cassiano's dead body collapse on the floor.

A woman screamed.

TRACY WATCHED Raven slash Cassiano La Bella's throat and saw the body fall. She was happy to let Raven have the kill. She wanted Harrison Hunt. Everything was the Texan's fault; if she wanted to avenge her late teammates, she had to eliminate him one way or another.

Simona Vadala started to cry and scream at the same time. Her reaction, and a sight Tracy caught out of the corner of one eye, tipped the scales in Tracy's favor. Raven's too. Even Roger Justice noticed.

Raven began walking back to the group, knife still in hand, blood dripping from the blade. Harrison Hunt stared at Raven, but Raven was watching Simona.

Simona slammed into one of the guards, executing an elbow strike to the guard's jaw. The guard grunted and started to raise his arms to block another strike; she wasn't strong enough to knock him down. Disabling the guard wasn't her goal. She wanted his Uzi, and with his arms up, she wrenched the weapon from his grasp. Shoving a now startled Hunt aside, she raised the Uzi at Raven.

A shot cracked overhead. The bullet split Simona's skull. Bits of her splashed Hunt, who recoiled back. Roger attacked the guard Simona struck and punched him again, grabbing the pistol from the man's holster. He fired into the guard's chest, then raised the weapon to the next one nearest him. Another shot. The guard dropped. Hunt started to run, cutting in front of Roger, forcing the last two guards to shuffle as they angled for a clear target. Another pair of bursts from above cut the last two guards down.

The echo of the gunfire rang loudly, but the white-coated watches from the walkway opposite yelled for more help. Raven ran to Tracy and Roger. Jack Moss remained a threat, and he broke into a sprint for the stairwell leading to the walkway above.

Raven and Tracy grabbed Uzis from the dead guards. Tracy took off after Hunt, while Raven ran after Jack Moss. Roger followed Tracy to cover her.

Moss fired at Raven as he started up a spiral staircase, the shot going wide. Raven held his fire until he reached the steps. Moss spun around, the arc of his pistol sweeping to Raven's chest. Raven fired the Uzi and punched holes in Moss's chest that spit back blood. Moss fell forward and tumbled toward Raven, who stepped to the side until Moss stopped. He continued upward.

He reached the walkway and waved to the two at the other end. Lia and Darbo, both crouched low, looking for further targets. How they'd entered the underground complex he didn't yet know, but he was glad they'd turned up. Raven trained his Uzi on the escaping, white-coated nuclear engineers on the opposite walkway. They'd had no problems building a weapon of mass destruction. He fired a burst, aiming for their legs. He wasn't going for kill shots. He needed them alive—or at least one or two—to tell of what had taken place at Hunt's direction, because he knew Harrison Hunt wasn't going to last more than a few seconds.

One of the engineers fell from a bullet in the left leg. The other stopped and raised their hands. Raven held his fire.

Tracy ran hard after Hunt as he ran down the extended

tunnel. She raised the Uzi to fire. Two guards entered from the other end and yelled for him to get out of the way. Tracy's first burst took down the guard who spoke, while her second tore away a chunk of the other's stomach as he tried to drive out of the way. Tracy shifted her aim back to Hunt, who had fallen to the floor, and was staring back at her as she took aim. She fired and didn't take her finger off the trigger. The burst stitched Hunt from chest to neck to face and left his body a bloody heap on the concrete floor.

KILLING Hunt took the fight out of everybody who remained —which numbered less than a dozen. Engineers, control room operators, a few leftover guards. Raven and his team corralled them in the center of the assembly room. Roger found a package of zip ties, and they used them to restrain Hunt's people. Then the team gathered to talk about what to do next.

It was Tracy who decided they should alert Clark Wilson at the CIA and let him call the Texas Rangers or the FBI or the Boy Scouts of whoever else he wanted to send. To make sure Wilson believed what Tracy told him, she took pictures with her cell phone. Pictures of the facility, the nukes, everything. Even what remained of Harrison Hunt.

Lia and Darbo remained on the upper walkway because Darbo's injuries prevented him from moving around. Raven returned to them and found him sitting against the wall, looking rough, breathing hard, Lia standing over him. Raven didn't feel great himself. He stopped and eased onto the floor beside Darbo.

"You getting lazy or something?" Raven said.

"I feel like a truck hit me."

"I'm glad you showed up when you did."

Lia said, "We found another tunnel. It brought us to the launch room." She gestured behind her.

Darbo said, "Where did you learn to use a knife like that? It was a cool fight."

"Long story. I'll teach you sometime."

Lia helped Raven to his feet. He wanted to find Tracy. Down below, he located her in the tunnel, standing over Hunt's body. A large puddle had pooled under him. He had an idea why she was still there.

He put a hand on her shoulder. "You okay?"

She nodded, but her face didn't communicate the message. She looked lost. "I'm not sure I care what happens next," she said.

"I'll stay with you until it's settled," he told her.

She rested a hand on top of his.

A LOOT AT BOOK TWELVE: THE DARK PASSAGE

In the lethal world of espionage thrillers, Sam Raven is once again the last line of defense. This time, the threat isn't just criminal—it's geopolitical.

When a tortured CIA operative is pulled from a Balkan cartel compound, Sam Raven leads a daring rescue that plunges him into Eastern Europe's deadliest underworld. There, he uncovers a chilling plot: a synthetic opioid designed for mass addiction, set to flood Europe. Behind it is a brutal cartel boss with plans to weaponize the profits, topple governments, and create a terrorist stronghold.

Raven joins forces with the rescued agent, Elena Covaci—a woman fueled by vengeance for war crimes committed during the Yugoslav Wars. But her personal mission may jeopardize the operation.

From Montenegro's jagged coastlines to the darkest corners of the Balkans, Raven battles betrayal, bloodshed, and a ticking clock. In this war, mercy is a weakness—and one wrong move could ignite a global crisis.

AVAILABLE DECEMBER 2025

ABOUT THE AUTHOR

A twenty-five year veteran of radio and television broadcasting, Brian Drake has spent his career in San Francisco where he's filled writing, producing, and reporting duties with stations such as KPIX-TV, KCBS, KQED, among many others. Currently carrying out sports and traffic reporting duties for Bloomberg 960, Brian Drake spends time between reports and carefully guarded morning and evening hours cranking out action/adventure tales.

A love of reading when he was younger inspired him to create his own stories, and he sold his first short story, "The Desperate Minutes," to an obscure webzine when he was 25 (more years ago than he cares to remember, so don't ask).

Brian Drake lives in California with his wife and two cats, and when he's not writing he is usually blasting along the back roads in his Corvette with his wife telling him not to drive so fast, but the engine is so loud he usually can't hear her.

briandrakebooks.com